"THIS IS A̶N̶N̶I̶E̶.̶ ̶S̶H̶E̶'̶L̶L̶ ̶B̶E̶ STAYING WITH US FOR A WEEK."

The staff crowded around to have a look, and Annie found herself in the thick of black uniforms and white aprons, polished shoes and curious faces.

"Miss." Were they bowing to *her,* to a little orphan named Annie? Leapin' lizards!

"And her dog Sandy," said Miss Farrell graciously.

"Who'll be staying with *me,*" said Annie, and everyone laughed.

"You're our guest, Annie," said Miss Farrell. "We'll take care of you. You're to have new clothing, and Cecille will help you dress and comb your hair. There will be bubbles in your bathtub, and clean satin sheets on your bed. When you've decided what you want to eat, you shall have it for your next meal, whatever it is."

The saucers of Annie's eyes grew to the size of dinner plates.

COLUMBIA PICTURES PRESENTS
A RAY STARK PRODUCTION
A JOHN HUSTON FILM

ANNIE

Starring
ALBERT FINNEY
CAROL BURNETT
BERNADETTE PETERS
ANN REINKING
TIM CURRY
GEOFFREY HOLDER
EDWARD HERRMANN as "F.D.R."
"SANDY" as himself
and Introducing AILEEN QUINN as "Annie"
Executive Producer JOE LAYTON
Choreography by ARLENE PHILLIPS
Music Adapted by RALPH BURNS
Production Executive HOWARD PINE
Supervising Editor MARGARET BOOTH, A.C.E.
Director of Photography RICHARD MOORE, A.S.C.
Music by CHARLES STROUSE
Lyrics by MARTIN CHARNIN
Screenplay by CAROL SOBIESKI
Produced by RAY STARK
Directed by JOHN HUSTON
From RASTAR
Original soundtrack album on Columbia records and tapes.

The stage play "Annie" was originally presented on the New
York Stage by Mike Nichols. Produced on the New York Stage
by Irwin Meyer, Stephen R. Friedman, and Lewis Allen. Book
of the stage play by Thomas Meehan—Music of the stage play
by Charles Strouse—Lyrics of the stage play by Martin Charnin.

Annie

Leonore Fleischer

**Based upon a screenplay
by Carol Sobieski**

BALLANTINE BOOKS • NEW YORK

Library of Congress Catalog Card Number: 82-1686

ISBN 0-345-26278-6

Manufactured in the United States of America

First Edition: June 1982

First special printing: August 1982

*Dedicated with affection to
my dear niece, Gloria Wilkinson*

CHAPTER ONE

Every night, just before she fell asleep, Annie would snuggle down in her warm bed and listen to the murmur of her parents' voices outside her bedroom door. Her drowsy eyes, not yet accustomed to the darkness, would drift slowly around the room, making a last-minute catalog of all her favorite things. Although she couldn't see the pictures on the walls, she had them memorized—Little Jack Horner, pulling a plum out of a brimming pie; Jack-Be-Nimble, leaping over a candlestick with a wavery flame; Little Miss Muffet, jumping up from her tuffet as the spider leered at her; Bo Peep, crying over her lost sheep, not noticing that they were gamboling toward her over the hills. Those dear familiar pictures had been there ever since Annie was a baby; her mother wanted to change them for something a little more suitable to Annie's ten years, but Annie didn't want to let them go. On the shelves across from the bed, Annie could make out the dim outlines of her dolls and books, her beloved stuffed animals, and the other toys that were crowded together so tightly they threatened to push each other off.

In the far corner stood the favorite toy of all—Annie's rocking horse, as gaily painted as a circus pony, tall and proud and very handsome. Annie would pretend that he was real, and that she could ride him out the front door, through the park, over the hills, and far away.

On the other side of the door, in the cozy living room, Annie's mother and father talked quietly together; Annie could barely hear them, and she couldn't really make out the words, but she kept catching the word "she" and occasionally the word "Annie," and she knew that they were talking about her, making plans for her future—college,

1

maybe. It made her feel so warm and safe that her eyes fluttered shut.

She loved them so much! Her beautiful, patient, loving mother, whose hands were soft. Her hair was brushed back from her face and pulled into a neat roll at the nape of her neck. Not marcelled or brilliantined, or cut short like a flapper's. Sometimes Annie would watch her brushing it; her mother's hair fell to her waist, a chestnut brown, with one or two strands of silvery gray. And her father, not very tall, not very handsome, but with a merry, laughing face and a mop of riotous red, curly hair that no barber could tame. And strong, very strong—he could pick Annie up as though she were little more than a rag doll and swing her around.

If she kept very quiet and pretended to be asleep, sooner or later her door would open and Annie's mother would come in to check on the little girl. She'd straighten the covers and touch Annie's brow, feeling for a sudden fever which was never there. But Annie must lie very still, and not touch back. Above all, she mustn't reach out her hand to touch back.

Now the door was opening, and a thin shaft of light from the hallway pierced the darkness. Annie screwed her eyes tightly shut and held her breath as her mother approached her bed. She could smell her mother's violet perfume and hear the rustle of her skirt. And she swore to herself, *This time I won't touch back. I won't even try.*

But she couldn't help herself. She wanted so badly to touch the warm hand that was reaching out to her. She pulled her hand out from under the blanket and reached for her mother and . . .

. . . And the Dream dissolved. It always dissolved when Annie tried to touch it, leaving her cold and lonely and sitting on the windowsill of the third-floor bathroom of the Hudson Street Home for Girls, Established 1891. On the other side of the bathroom door was not a warm cozy bedroom filled with toys, but a bleak, cheerless, airless (unless you counted drafts) dormitory with iron cots for beds and orange crates for bureaus. And there was no mother, no father, nobody but fifty-nine other orphans and Miss Hannigan, their keeper.

Annie had never known her parents, had never known

any other home but the orphanage. Yet she was set apart from the other girls; Annie had her Dream. And one day the Dream would come true at last; didn't she have half a locket to prove it? When they left her at the Hudson Street Home ten years ago, there had been a note tucked in the basket with the redheaded baby. The note promised to whom it may concern that they, Annie's mother and father, would come back as soon as they could, as soon as times got better, to claim their baby Annie. As a token of their promise, half a locket on a chain was inside the envelope. They would keep the other half, said the note, so that everybody would recognize everybody when the great day came. So, strictly speaking, Annie was not an orphan. She had parents, half a locket, and a Dream.

Not that any of it mattered to Miss Hannigan. She was usually fair and impartial in her treatment of the orphans. She hated them all alike. Locket or no locket, parents or no parents, Dream or no Dream, you still scrubbed floors, washed, ironed, and folded laundry, went to bed hungry, and obeyed orders. If Miss Hannigan appeared to favor Annie with a little bit more of her hatred, it was only because Annie was smarter, tougher, bolder, and more independent than the fifty-nine other girls. In Annie, Miss Hannigan sensed a leader, and she detested leaders. Miserable troublemakers. Rotten kids.

Annie sighed and shifted on the bathroom window ledge. It was an uncomfortable and precarious perch, because the window was set up high in the wall, just under the ceiling. To reach it (and nobody but Annie had ever thought of reaching it) you had to stand on the toilet, climb up on the tank, and swing yourself up the hot-water pipe until you could hoist yourself up on the sill. But once there, you had the only privacy in the entire orphanage. Although the window was coated with decades of grime (it hadn't been washed since 1891 and this was now 1933), Annie had wiped a little place clean, and through it she could see the sky. In the winter, you could see a star or two and now and then a piece of the moon. In the summer, the sky was still blue, because the orphans went to bed before eight. Why not? They had to get up before six, didn't they? And what else was there for them to do? They had no books, no radio, no playthings of any

3

kind, no midnight snacks, no Mutt and Jeff or Popeye or Blondie, or anything else to make them smile.

If I try very hard, and keep my eyes tight shut, she told herself, *the Dream might come back. And this time I swear not to put my hand out.* Wrapping her skinny arms tightly around her skinny legs, Annie squinched her eyes shut and attempted to concentrate. Every one of the hundreds of freckles on her face stood out against the white skin with the effort. And the mop of red curls quivered. Although New York City was in the throes of a heat wave and the orphanage was stifling, the stone sill of the bathroom window was like a block of hard ice, and Annie shivered, glad she was wearing her ragged old red sweater over her faded hopsacking underwear. Once the fabric had been new, and had been either brown or gray, although why anybody wanted brown or gray material Annie could never figure out. Her own favorite color was red. But many years of wearing and washing had faded it out to a color neither brown nor gray, but combining the worst features of both. But Annie was used to the color. Most of the orphans slept in their underwear.

The red sweater, on the other hand, had never been new. It had come in the barrel. The Hudson Street Home for Girls was a favorite charity for a number of wealthy society women. Not that they visited there, oh, my, no. Not that they donated money. But twice a year, these society ladies held meetings. In the spring, their chauffeurs carried to the meeting every scrap of castoff and unwanted clothing which their own daughters had outgrown. This clothing was packed up in a barrel and sent to the orphanage.

In the fall, the ladies met again, each one bringing a little gift or two for an orphan child's Christmas. These were new and often very pretty—dolls, books, games—the kinds of things so many little girls take for granted. These were beautifully wrapped and duly sent off to Miss Hannigan.

Now Miss Hannigan was a great believer in popular maxims: Spare the Rod and Spoil the Child being her favorite. But Waste Not, Want Not ran it a close second. Whenever the barrel filled with the secondhand clothing arrived, Miss Hannigan had it brought directly to her room. There she would open it eagerly and paw through the

4

jumble herself. Often the best things, destined for the older girls, wound up on her own back. Silk blouses, for example. What on earth would an orphan want with silk? You can't wear silk while scrubbing floors, can you? Then the barrel was carefully repacked and stowed away in Miss Hannigan's locked supply room.

At Christmas, long limousines would drive up to the Hudson Street Home for Girls, and chauffeurs in black uniforms and caps with shiny patent bills would bring in stacks of gaily wrapped boxes. The orphans' eyes would grow round with excitement and anticipation, then droop in disappointment as the boxes disappeared behind Miss Hannigan's bolted doors.

Every single box would be unwrapped by Miss Hannigan, ever so carefully, so as not to tear the tissue paper or muss the silver and gold ribbons. Then the presents would be stacked in their store boxes along one wall, waiting for Miss Hannigan to take them back to the stores right after Christmas and get her money back. Oh, Miss Hannigan loved Christmas! *Such* a jolly time!

Then, *one* object from the used-clothing barrel would be wrapped up in the gift paper and tied with the gift ribbons and marked with an orphan's name. Useful things, like an old middy blouse with a faded blue tie, or a pinafore with a daisy appliqué and indelible ink stains down the front. Or somebody's old red sweater, wearing thin at the elbows. What else did an orphan need? They might not have gotten even these things (there being a lively market for good used clothing) except for the fact that the society ladies liked to receive thank-you notes for their lovely Christmas presents from the grateful orphans. Every year, Miss Hannigan saw to it that every child wrote the identical ambiguous note: Dear Mrs. Rockesmeller, Thank you so much for the beautiful present. I shall always treasure it and remember your generosity. Sincerely yours, Clara Churchmouse, Hudson Street Home for Girls, Established 1891.

It was a hard-knock life, no two ways about it. Outside the orphanage, things weren't all that wonderful either. The world had been on a free ride for ten years, ever since the Great War in Europe, in which so many men had died in order to end all wars forever. In a fever of optimism, Americans had plunged heavily into the stock market, buying, buying and never selling. The price of stocks soared, way above their actual value, yet people kept on buying. Women shortened their hair and their skirts. The waltz went out and hot jazz came in. You couldn't buy a bottle of whiskey legally, but you could buy it illegally on every street corner. Men plastered their hair down like Rudy Valentino and called themselves sheiks, and their dancing partners shebas. Everybody was having a wonderful time, doing the Charleston on the brink of a volcano.

And then the volcano erupted, and the stock market came tumbling down with a Crash that was heard around the world. Overnight, fortunes were wiped out, men and women thrown out of work, factories shut down. Everybody stopped singing "Boop Boop Be Doop" and started singing "Brother, Can You Spare a Dime?" The Great Depression set in. Stockbrokers jumped out of their office windows; men without work went on the bum and lived in hobo jungles. Other men sold apples two-for-a-nickel on street corners. Veterans, who had been promised a bonus that never materialized in cash, marched on Washington to protest, and were shot at by General Douglas MacArthur and his troops. Times were hard.

By 1932, everybody was so sick of the depression that they did what Americans always do. They blamed it on the president, Herbert Hoover, went to the polls and voted the other party in by a landslide. In this case, they elected a Democrat, Franklin Delano Roosevelt, former governor of New York, former secretary of the Navy. FDR, as he was called (he was called other things by the Republicans), promised a New Deal, with jobs for everybody. No more soup kitchens, no more breadlines, only work and a worker's pay. Things were starting to look a little better, and America began to cheer up. They sang: "Just around the corner, there's a rainbow in the sky. So let's have another cup of coffee, and let's have another piece of pie." They sang: "Who's afraid of the big, bad wolf?" and they meant the depression, which was starting to lift a little.

Lifting outside the Hudson Street Home for Girls, that is. Inside, things were as gloomy as they always were. Terrible food, and never enough of it. Freezing cold in the winter, hotter than a stove in the summer. And never ever was there a spring or a fall.

In theory, life shouldn't have been as bad as it was. According to the state laws governing the orphanage, the girls were supposed to be well schooled, with classes five hours a day. They were supposed to learn English, spelling, geography, arithmetic, music, history, bookkeeping. They were supposed to have two hours of gym and one of art appreciation every week.

In practice, the only school Miss Hannigan believed in was the School of Hard Knocks. She had struck up a deal with the local laundry; they would deliver huge bundles of dirty sheets, towels and tablecloths, and the orphan girls would scrub them clean in huge tubs on washboards, put them through the mangle, hang them on the line, take them down and fold them, or press them out on huge ironing boards with heavy irons that weren't electric. These duties kept the girls much too busy for school, but it put a nice piece of change into Miss Hannigan's pocket.

In theory, any one of the girls could be adopted into a good home at any time. Orphans were always up for adoption, always dreaming of adoption, longing for a mother and a father and a home, yearning for the things that other children took for granted—enough food to eat, a warm place to sleep, a tender hand, a little love, an end to loneliness.

In practice, forget it! Any orphan over the age of three didn't have a chance, unless she was blessed with dimples and curls like Shirley Temple. Prospective parents were interested in something pink and white and tiny, not in a scrawny, big-eyed, hungry girl with scabs on her knees from scrubbing floors and knuckles rubbed raw on the washboard.

In theory, the board of directors of the Hudson Street Home for Girls was supposed to make regular visits to determine if the girls were being well treated, well educated, and well fed. Welfare was their concern, and they weren't cruel men.

In practice, they were busy men, and the welfare of sixty little girls was not so pressing a concern as their business worries, especially now, with That Man in the White House. Besides, they placed implicit faith in Miss

7

Hannigan, who sent them glowing reports weekly. If anything, the girls were being spoiled with too much food, too much love, and too many presents. Kind Miss Hannigan, who worked so hard for such a small salary. However did she manage to make ends meet?

By feeding sixty little girls mush, in watered-down portions.

Annie's blue eyes were tightly closed, and she thought she could feel the Dream almost beginning again. If only she could get it back. On this hot night, it was impossible to sleep; better to stay up here and hope for the best.

"Annie! *Annie!* ANNIE!"

Annie's eyes snapped open as she heard Molly screaming. The poor baby must be having another one of her nightmares; the screaming had turned into frightened sobbing. Annie caught hold of the water pipe and slithered down, running into the dormitory.

Little Molly, the youngest in the room at six, was thrashing around on her bed and crying. Tears had plastered her dark hair to her cheeks and her nose was running, but she still held tightly to her precious doll, a faceless, shapeless lump of beloved rag.

By now, Molly's sobs had wakened the other orphans, who were sitting up and rubbing their eyes. Pepper, the oldest at thirteen, and mean as a snake, was standing on her bed, her hands knotted into fists and placed squarely on her hips.

"How am I supposed to get any sleep around here?" she demanded, furious, as Annie ran to Molly's side, and gathered the little girl in her arms. "Shhhhhh. It's all right, Molly. I'm here. Everything's all right."

"Molly shouldn't be in this room!" shouted Pepper angrily. "She's a baby! She cries all the time! She wets the bed!"

"I d—d—d—do not!" hiccoughed Molly through her tears.

"Shhhh, blow!" ordered Annie, finding a crumpled handkerchief in her sweater pocket. Molly obediently blew her nose with a loud honk, and Annie mopped at her eyes.

Duffy, ten, but a head smaller than Annie, turned

8

ferociously on Pepper. She loathed a bully, and Pepper was a bully.

"You're the one who shouldn't be in here!" she yelled.

"Yeah!" July chimed in, protective of Molly. "You're the one always making all the noise!" July was eight years old, and tagged along after Annie and Duffy like a small, chubby shadow. She had been left at the orphanage as an infant, with a note pinned to her blanket, saying: "Hear's our dotter July. Pleas take god kare of her." Probably, they meant "Julie," but July she was named and July she was called, like the month. She told anybody who would listen that she was born on the Fourth of July, and if Miss Hannigan had permitted birthdays in the orphanage, that's when they would have celebrated it.

"We're gonna get in trouble," Kate moaned, rolling her eyes. Noise like this always brought Miss Hannigan on the double. At this hour of the night, gin would have made Miss Hannigan unsteady on her pins, but with their luck she'd be able to walk.

"Yeah!" Duffy agreed with Kate. "So shut up, Pepper!"

"You shut up!" bawled Pepper.

With a low growl like a feisty little pup, Duffy took a running jump at Pepper, landing on her with both fists flying, although the older girl stood a good six inches higher and outweighed her by about twenty-five pounds. July, with the instincts of a born follower, raced after Duffy and began to pound Pepper with her pillow. Noise and feathers rose to the heavens.

Molly had stopped crying and watched the fight with a mixture of childish wonder and glee. Tessie, small, dark, and nervous, took a strand of hair into her mouth and began chewing on it, her unbreakable habit when things went from bad to worse.

"Oh, my goodness, oh, my goodness," she muttered through the wet ends of her hair. She burrowed under her pillow in terror.

Before the battle could escalate, Annie's hard little hands were forcing the combatants apart, pushing them away from one another, confiscating July's pillow.

"Cut it out!" she hissed through her teeth. "I mean it!" Annie's small, freckled face wore a look of intense ferocity. "You want Miss Hannigan to come in here?" She gave

9

Duffy a push. "Go back to bed. Now." Then she turned to Pepper, who backed down. "Or you'll have me to deal with."

The fight was over. Muttering, the girls obeyed, climbing back into their own beds, settling down again to sleep.

Molly gave a little whimper as Annie tucked her in.

"I can't sleep, Annie," she said with a tremble in her voice. She had been orphaned only two of her six years, and she couldn't adjust to the harshness of orphanage life.

"I know," whispered Annie sympathetically, smoothing the child's dark hair back over her forehead. "Sometimes it's hard. Close your eyes. Think about your folks."

Molly's grubby little fingers reached up to touch the precious locket dangling from Annie's neck. "You're the only one who really has folks," she said sadly. "Mine are dead."

Annie gave the little girl a quick hug. "Think about the folks who are gonna adopt you. Because they want a little girl with brown hair and brown eyes."

Molly was still young enough to believe, and now she shut her eyes. "Sing something, Annie," she begged. "Please? Sing 'Minnie the Moocher.' Please, Annie. It will help me sleep."

Annie laughed and nodded. "Minnie the Moocher" was her specialty, learned from stolen visits to Miss Hannigan's radio when Miss Hannigan was out returning orphan presents to the department stores. " 'Folks, here's the story of Minnie the Moocher,' " she sang to Molly, rocking the little girl in her arms. But before she could get to the part about Minnie's heart being as big as a whale, the door was flung open with a bang and the overhead light shed a harsh and sickly glare over the iron cots and the few pitiful belongings in the orange crates by the beds.

"Did I hear *singing* in here?" rasped a horridly familiar voice. Miss Hannigan!

Once upon a time Miss Hannigan had probably been a little girl, not too different from the orphans, but it was hard to picture her with a mother and a father and a first name. She appeared to have been born mean, skinny, blowsy, and drunk. Life might have dealt severe disappointments to Miss Hannigan; perhaps she had wanted a home, a husband, and some children of her own. Perhaps.

Or maybe she liked things exactly as they were, sixty little girls living in mortal fear of her. Certainly, she made the most of it at every opportunity.

Yet, Miss Hannigan had her good side. She drank. While other ladies filled their bathtubs with sweet-smelling bubbles, Miss Hannigan filled hers with gin. Foul-smelling, poisonous gin which she manufactured herself in the tub, a leftover from Prohibition days, when gin was hard to come by. By now, she was used to the hideous concoction, and had even come to like it. Several dozen gallons of wood alcohol, a few juniper berries, stir once or twice, let it age slowly overnight and it would start to eat its way right through the tub. Because she drank, Miss Hannigan was frequently drunk. Sometimes she was kind enough to pass out, and the orphans lived for those times. When Miss Hannigan was passed out and snoring, the Hudson Street Home for Girls, Established 1891, knew its only few moments of peace. They were moments worth celebrating, and celebrate the orphans did. They would listen to Miss Hannigan's radio, and dance to the music (both were strictly forbidden at other times). It was from the forbidden radio that Annie had learned of President Roosevelt and the New Deal. The orphans were not allowed newspapers or any other word from the outside world. Or they would go through Miss Hannigan's pile of discarded magazines and rotogravure sections, which she sold to the junk dealer when she was through with them. It was in one of these magazines, the *Woman's Home Companion,* that Annie had seen a picture of the room in her Dream, complete with the nursery-rhyme pictures on the wall and the rocking horse in the corner.

Yes, the orphans could be very fond of Miss Hannigan, when she was asleep and snoring. But it was the phase before she passed out that they hated and feared the most. Because Miss Hannigan could be a very mean drunk.

She was in the mean-drunk phase now; every girl in the room felt the marrow of her bones congeal in terror. A bottle half filled with homemade gin swung from Miss Hannigan's hand as she went marching unsteadily through the bedroom, shrieking her anger.

"Get out of bed! This room's a mess!" she yelled, tugging the frightened and unwilling girls out of their cots.

"Who said you could move the beds?" she screamed as she noticed the girls had pushed their cots closer together for what little companionship they could get. "This room's going to be regulation by breakfast, my little pig droppings, or kill! kill! *kill!*"

"It's the middle of the night," protested Annie. A bony hand, covered in cheap glittery rings, with long blood-red fingernails, grabbed her by the collar of her undershirt and yanked her off the bed. They stood nose to nose for an instant, and Annie was nearly overcome by the mingled odors of cheap perfume and stale gin. "And if the floor doesn't shine like the top of the Chrysler building, your backside will!"

Hissing with fury, Miss Hannigan gave Annie such a push that the child went stumbling backward and fell to the floor. Now she glared around the room to make certain that everybody was up and dressing. "Understand?" she demanded.

"Yes, Miss Hannigan," chorused the orphans reluctantly. All except Annie, who was muttering something under her breath, stopping as she caught Miss Hannigan's glaring eye.

Miserable little troublemaker! Rotten kid! "What do we say, Annie?" prompted Miss Hannigan with a vicious leer.

Annie hesitated for a fraction of a moment, then gave in. "I love you, Miss Hannigan," she sing-songed through clenched teeth. Those five words had been drilled into her, into all the orphans, over the years. "I love you, Miss Hannigan." Did the woman think the words were true just because she commanded them to be spoken?

But the woman seemed satisfied now. With a complacent nod, she took another long pull at the gin bottle and headed for the door, shaking her head. "Why any kid would want to be an orphan is beyond me."

Annie stood looking after her. That tears it, she thought. Enough is enough, and I've had enough. Standing still and closing your eyes wasn't the way to have a Dream come true. It was time to go out looking for the Dream. It was time to run away again.

CHAPTER TWO

Annie had always been caught, every time she'd run away. Caught and brought back and punished. But it never stopped her from trying again. Because someday she'd make it, bust loose and get free and find her mother and father. They'd know each other on account of the locket, and they'd be so happy to see her, and they'd have the best excuse in the world why they hadn't shown up, and they'd all live happily together, and they'd agree to adopt Molly.

The reason she'd always been caught is that she'd never had a plan. On impulse, she would slip out the front door when it was opened and head down the street, running hard until she was caught. Why, that wasn't even running away, that was exercise! But now she had a kind of plan, and it involved her getting away clean. As clean as dirty laundry could be, that is.

There wasn't a lot of coming and going at the orphanage; it wasn't exactly a hot social center. Every two weeks, the man from the shirtwaist factory came with large bolts of cloth to be turned into blouses, skirts, and dresses on sewing machines. He subcontracted out a number of his contracts, and one of his suppliers was the Hudson Street Home for Girls, Established 1891. Miss Hannigan had set up a little sweatshop in what should have been the schoolroom. Instead of desks, there were sewing and pressing machines, dressmakers' dummies, ironing boards, and cutting tables. Miss Hannigan claimed that she was teaching the older girls a trade and a skill that could not be obtained for money elsewhere, but every penny made on the sewing found its way into her rusty old leatherette pocketbook. Between the laundry and the dressmaking, the Hudson Street Home brought in a tidy little profit, which Miss

13

Hannigan made tidy use of. She spent it on alcohol for the bathtub and lavalieres of brass and cheap glass beads, kimonos of artificial silk, printed with large, sleazy flowers, red hair dye, sling-back mules trimmed with marabou feathers, and a monkey-fur jacket. Miss Hannigan agreed with the French saying: It Is Necessary to Suffer to Be Beautiful. That is to say, she didn't think it was necessary for *her* to suffer, only the orphans.

Every week, on Wednesday, Mr. Bundles came from the laundry to deliver the dirty sheets, towels, and tablecloths for the orphans to wash, and to take away their dirty sheets (they had no towels and, needless to say, no tablecloths) for *him* to wash. It was an odd arrangement, forced on Miss Hannigan by the board of directors, who paid the laundry bills themselves, and who would wonder if there were nothing to pay.

By the time the orphans had scrubbed down the walls and the staircases, the floors and the kitchen, it was Wednesday morning, time to strip the beds for Mr. Bundles. Laundry was piled into a large cart, which was wheeled to the front door and up a ramp into Mr. Bundles' truck. And that was Annie's plan, so simple it was pure genius. She would hide in the laundry and be carried out right under Miss Hannigan's nose.

"Oh, my goodness, oh, my goodness," gasped Tessie when she saw Annie climb into the laundry cart and, holding her nose, duck down underneath the dirty, smelly sheets.

"They'll put you in the cellar with the ghosts," exclaimed Kate. She was the one with the vivid imagination.

"You'll get whipped again," warned Duffy.

"You're gonna get us in trouble!" wailed July.

Molly burst into tears as she saw Annie disappear under the sheets.

"Shut up, Molly," urged Annie, her voice muffled by linen.

Pepper thrust her lower lip out. "I'm gonna tell."

"And I'll rearrange your teeth," threatened the laundry cart.

Molly's sobbing came to an abrupt stop as Miss Hannigan, loaded for bear, came stalking in to chivvy her charges.

"What are you standing around for?" she snarled at the suddenly silent girls. "You have to do the kitchen and the bathroom before lunch, my little pig droppings, and if you skip the corners, there will *be* no lunch." At the gasp of dismay that arose from the orphans, an evil little smile broke out over her face. "And we're not having hot mush today," she purred.

Spontaneous applause, cheers, and whistles, cries of joy.

"We're having *cold* mush," she cackled, enjoying her cruel joke.

A chorus of groans and gripes rose to her ears, past the long, glitzy earrings. *"What!?"* she roared, suddenly furious.

"We love you, Miss Hannigan," they piped obediently.

Miss Hannigan's hackles subsided. "Wonderful," she said flatly. Then, as the new thought struck her, she looked around. "Where's Annie?" she demanded. That little troublemaker. Rotten kid.

"She had to go bafroom," answered Molly, inspired.

"She had to go bafroom," mocked Miss Hannigan in a disbelieving lisp. "Oh, yeah? Well then, why . . . ?"

But her suspicions were interrupted by the announcement that the laundryman was here with his truck.

"Oooohh!" squeaked Miss Hannigan, transformed into a breathy young girl at the mere idea of a man, any man. "It's Mr. Bundles!" And with a pat at her dyed and ratted hair, she was off down the stairs to the street.

As quickly as they could, Duffy and July bumped the laundry cart down the staircase (it yelled *Ow!* twice) and out into the street behind Miss Hannigan.

Mr. Bundles was unloading an empty laundry cart to leave when Miss Hannigan came dancing up, frolicsome as a gazelle, but ten times clumsier.

Oh, boy, he muttered unhappily under his breath. *She's in one of them moods. Better get outta here fast.*

Miss Hannigan batted her eyelashes so hard a bead of mascara flew through the air and spattered on Mr. Bundles' white uniform.

The pupils of Miss Hannigan's eyes now narrowed in suspicion as she saw Duffy trying to push the laundry cart up the ramp to the panel truck.

"I'm trying to help you," Duffy called back, her face a mask of sweating innocence. As Mr. Bundles came over to give the child a hand, Duffy muttered in an undertone, "It's heavy today."

"It sure is," grunted Bundles, putting his shoulder to it. "It feels like . . ." Duffy dug a quick elbow into his ribs to warn him, but it was too late. Miss Hannigan was stalking over, frowning.

"Like what?" she demanded. "Let me see in there."

In a flash, Mr. Bundles caught on to what was . . . *who* was in the cart.

Duffy gave the cart a final shove into the truck.

"Until next week, Miss Hannigan," and he kissed his hand to her.

Miss Hannigan melted, and her eyelids fluttered like a butterfly in love. "Adieu, my little whippet lips," she trilled throatily. "Adieu." And she floated back into the orphanage.

From the window above, Tessie, Kate, and Molly watched the laundry truck clatter away down the cobbled street and turn a corner.

"Oh, my goodness, oh, my goodness," squeaked Tessie, chewing on her hair in excitement.

"Juju beans! She made it!" called out Kate.

And poor little Molly burst into tears. Who would sing to her tonight? Who would comfort her when she had nightmares?

Scram sighed as he turned the corner and saw the boys standing in front of the butcher shop. This wasn't his lucky day. He hadn't eaten a bite since the day before yesterday, and he was feeling weak and light-headed. But even in his enfeebled condition he could tell that those boys spelled trouble. And in front of that butcher shop, too. His luck was running *all* bad. Not that the butcher was the most generous of men, but in the past he had parted with a scrap or a bone, and sometimes, around the garbage cans in the alley behind the shop, Scram had found a mouthful or two, not the best quality, perhaps, but then Scram had never eaten a mouthful of the best quality.

But with those mean-looking boys standing there—four of them—it wasn't worth the risk. Or was it? Scram took one step forward, then two steps back, then decided against it. He'd go back the way he'd come, and try again later.

But it was already too late. He'd been spotted. The boys were running across the street toward him, shouting. Scram turned tail and ran for his life.

He couldn't run very fast in his present condition; he ran like a wheezing old dog. Actually, he wasn't old in years, just old in the ways of the streets. Experienced, or he wouldn't have survived even this long. A dog without a license in a city without a heart—that was almost as bad as . . . as . . . being an orphan. And why, as Miss Hannigan would say, why would anyone ever want to be an orphan? Or a stray dog?

A stone bounced off Scram's furry shoulder, and he ran harder. No fair. Stones weren't fair. Sticks weren't fair. Tin cans tied to the tail weren't fair. But they all seemed to be Scram's lot in life. If only he could accept it philosophically!

He was a dog without a home, without anybody to love or be loved by, without even a name. "Scram" was what most people called him, but he also answered to "Beat-It" and to "Get-the-Heck-Outta-Here." If by answering, you meant running away. Scram lived by his wits, sleeping under cars, shivering in alleys in the winter, drinking out of puddles and open hydrants, scrounging his food wherever he could find it. He wasn't a large dog and he wasn't a small dog. He didn't have any real color to his fur, and his lineage was as undistinguished as he was. He was your basic nondescript mutt, and the only striking thing about him was his eyes—which were large and soft and brown and miserable.

He couldn't do tricks, but he was smart. And brave. And loyal. And, had he but known it, loving. But these were qualities that seemed little in demand these days. Scotties were the big favorite—even President Roosevelt had a Scottie, Fala, who lived in the White House and probably ate filet mignon off golden plates. Scotties and cocker spaniels, poodles and chows, bull terriers—these were the popular and fashionable dogs. Even wirehairs were big. There was a little wirehair in Scram, a couple of generations back. But not enough to make somebody pick him up and give him a home.

17

Scram looked back over his shoulder as he fled down the alley. No doubt about it, the gang of boys was gaining on him.

The laundry truck bumped over the cobblestones, and the carts in the back went pitching this way and that. Buried under the sheets, Annie fought to get her head out, but just as she was almost free, another bump sent her flying back into the washbasket. *I'm not gonna live through this,* she thought, *but just in case I do, and I get away, it will be worth it.* But she was getting sick to her stomach, with all the pitching and rolling. It was like crossing the Atlantic in a January gale on a ship with no stabilizers.

At last, at the very moment when Annie was glad she'd missed lunch, Mr. Bundles pulled over to the curb and stopped. A minute later, he was setting Annie down on the sidewalk, where she wobbled unsteadily until she got her land legs back. Then, with a wide grin and a wave of thanks, she was on her way.

On her way where? She had no idea, but the late-summer day was so beautiful, the streets so lively and bustling, that merely to walk down them gave her a sense of well-being and a feeling of freedom. All she knew was that she was somewhere on the West Side of Manhattan, walking uptown away from Hudson Street.

New York in 1933 was very different from what it is today. For one thing, there were far fewer automobiles, and many businesses—small ones, admittedly—were conducted by horse and wagon or even by pushcart. Television hadn't been invented, and people looked out of their windows for entertainment. There were no transistor radios, but organ grinders wandered around with little monkeys on their leashes, playing for pennies. Knife sharpeners carried large grindstones on wheelbarrows, calling out for housewives to bring down their knives to sharpen, a nickel apiece. "I cash clothes! I cash clothes!" sang the old-clothes men in the back alleys. They'd climb up six flights of stairs to pay a dime for a wornout overcoat, or a penny for a pair of shoes.

Kids were everywhere, playing in the streets, dodging the traffic. They played stoopball, and stickball, with manhole covers for bases. They played King, a neighborhood variety of handball. They played Giant Steps and Puss-in-the-Corner and King of the Mountain. They threw mumblety-peg and shot marbles and spun tops. Rope-skipping was very popular, because the only equipment you needed was a piece of clothesline, and Double Dutch was the killer game, only for the best rope-jumpers. Annie had never done any of these things, and she was fascinated. She wanted to stop and watch; she wanted to join in, but her instincts told her she'd better keep going. So she wandered on, in no direction in particular.

There is one other difference between the New York of then and now that's worth mentioning. Today, the police ride around in squad cars, two to a car. In those days, a single cop walked a beat, looking for anything and anybody who excited his suspicion. And, generally, a cop knew every man, woman, and even child on his beat.

Officer McVie watched from across the street as a small redheaded girl clambered down from a laundry truck. Here was somebody he'd never seen before, somebody who was too pale for a kid this time of year, like she'd been kept indoors a lot. Somebody in a faded old dress too big for her and an old red sweater too small for her. Somebody with an institutional look about her, who was gazing too curiously at commonplace people and ordinary occupations, as though she'd never seen them before. No other business was pressing the policeman at this moment; so he took off after Annie, keeping out of her sight but dogging her half a block behind.

Annie turned a corner and came upon a street market, pushcart after pushcart selling old clothes, pickled herring, watches and rings of "real gold," men's hats, cages of live pigeons, mounds of dead chickers, secondhand books in Yiddish, Greek, Italian, German, even Chinese. Fascinated, she slowed down, and behind her, the policeman slowed down, too. He was on to something; he was certain of that now. This kid had escaped from a jail of some kind. He could tell because now she was looking so happy, happier than any kid had a right to be with times to hard.

They caught up with him, as he'd known they would, trapping him against the wall in an alley. Scram had growled and barked, but the boys paid no attention. They knew he was all mouth; this dog wouldn't bite anybody. With a lot of pushing and jostling and yelling they managed to tie a long string to his tail, with three tin cans fastened to the string. Now when that mangy old dog ran away, the clattering behind him would scare him out of his wits and make him run faster. Boy, was this fun! It even beat grabbing shopping bags from angry old ladies. Spike, the oldest and largest of the group, gave Scram a whack on the behind that sent him running and yelping out of the alley, trying frantically to shake the cans loose from his tail. Howling with laughter, the boys took off in hot pursuit of the terrified dog.

The smell of the pickled herring and the garlic sausages hanging from their strings was beginning to get to Annie. Breakfast had been a tiny bowl of ice-cold mush, but even that would taste good to Annie now. She was starving, and the aroma of salami was making her mouth water. Of course, she didn't have a penny on her; well, actually, when did she ever have a penny on her? Time to move on, to arenas less fragrant and tantalizing.

As she passed the alley between the rows of houses, a frightened dog raced past her, his heart pounding, eyes staring, tongue panting. To his tail was attached a string of empty tin cans. Behind him hotfooted a gang of yelling boys. Annie shook her head in disgust. How some people got their kicks!

But as she moved past the alley on her way to somewhere else, a yelp of pain stopped her in her tracks. She peered into the alley's dimness. The gang of boys had the scruffy dog penned in a dead end, and two of them were holding him down while a third one was tightening the string around his tail. In pain, the dog kept biting at the string, turning and turning in terrified circles, as the noisy cans clattered on the cobbles behind him.

Annie marched into the alley and stood there watching, her hands on her hips. Although she was standing as tall as she knew how, she was still smaller than the smallest of the boys, and many inches smaller than their leader.

Who now stood watching the shabbily dressed little girl with a sneer on his face.

"Keep walking, kid," he told her scornfully.

Annie took another step toward him, then another.

"Bug off!" Spike ordered, getting annoyed.

"What's he ever done to you?" asked Annie, jerking a thumb at the cowering dog.

Spike glared at her menacingly. "You want a fat lip?" he inquired, not expecting an answer.

But Annie *did* come up with an answer. She kicked Spike in the shins, good and hard. Now he was *really* mad. Although he rarely beat up girls, except for his sister, he came at Annie with his fists clenched and head down, ready to wipe the alley floor with this nosy redheaded brat. "You little—" he began, but he never got a chance to tell Annie what creature he was comparing her to, because on the way there his jaw met Annie's hard little fist, and he was sent flying. Before he could even begin to recover from Annie's left, her right plowed into his stomach, and birdies began to go tweet-tweet around his head. He slumped to the cobbles with a peaceful look on his face.

The gang couldn't believe their eyes. Spike? Taken out by a girl? By a *little* girl? Gotta be some mistake, right?

But the little girl was turning to them now, fists cocked, eyes flashing, ready to take them all on. "Anybody else?" she was saying. "Then *get lost.*"

Now, of course, if they'd all rushed her at once, Annie wouldn't have stood a chance. But somehow that never occurred to any of them. What occurred to them was that they had business elsewhere, pressing business. It wasn't as though they were running away from a girl, right? Just because a fella's remembered an important engagement that required his presence elsewhere? One by one they turned tail and got lost, and within twenty-two seconds the alley was empty, except for Annie and Scram. Even Spike had recovered enough to slink away quickly, so he could pull his story together. He slipped, that was it. Slipped on the slimy cobbles just as he was about to deck the snotty little kid, and he hit his head and . . .

Annie knelt down and gently unfastened the cans from the dog's tail. He lay with his chin on the ground and his

21

paws over his nose. He was a mess. His fur was matted and dirty, and cuts showed through on his skin, where he'd been hit by rocks thrown by those crummy boys. His ribs were showing. What a loser!

"Okay, it's okay. They're gone now. You can take off. Nobody's gonna hurt ya," Annie told him, but the dog didn't move or take his eyes off her. Big brown eyes, the saddest eyes that Annie had ever seen, even sadder and browner than Molly's.

"Hey, you're all right. Go on now." And Annie gave him a little push. The dog gave a kind of sigh and a little shudder and settled closer to the ground.

Annie stood up and shook her head, amused. "Dumb dog. Well, cheer up. I gotta be going. So long."

She headed for the entrance to the alley. Behind her she heard a low whine, then the dog got up stiffly and came hobbling after her.

At the entrance to the alley, Scram caught up with Annie. He was grateful to her, of course, for taking on that gang and getting rid of his tormentors and his torment. But it was more than gratitude that was making him follow her. Scram could tell by the way she was dressed that this little redheaded girl couldn't stand him a meal, probably didn't have anything to eat herself. He knew there was no percentage in it for him. But none of that mattered. What mattered was that, when she was kneeling beside him, he'd looked into her face and that was *it*. A feeling of such love, such devotion had washed over him that it had pressed him to the ground, and he'd trembled and whined beneath it. This little girl was his destiny; she was his person for life. His canine fate had been decreed, and it couldn't be otherwise.

Not that he wished it otherwise. He'd never loved anybody in his life, not since he'd been a tiny puppy with a mother, and that was long ago. But this little freckle-faced, blue-eyed, redheaded girl belonged to him now, and nothing anybody would ever say or do would alter matters. He'd follow her to the ends of the earth, let alone the mouth of an alley.

Annie turned and smiled down at him, touching his flea-infested head with gentle fingers. "I can't find my own home. So how could I find yours?"

Scram wagged his tail happily, content only to hear Annie's voice. As she moved away from him, he followed.

"Dumb dog! Latch on to someone who can feed you. Give you a bath. Put something on those cuts. Go on now."

Scram, who never had done a trick in his life before, held up his paw for Annie to take.

The little girl shook her head impatiently. "You already told me thank you. I didn't do nothing any decent person wouldn'ta done."

Scram lifted both paws and sat up. Annie stopped dead, and turned to look at him. "You . . . are . . . embarrassing me," she said slowly and distinctly. "Now, *scram!*"

At the sound of his name on her lips, he did the only thing a gentleman could do in the circumstances. He licked her face, wetly and enthusiastically.

"Yuck!" yelled Annie, and turned and ran through the crowded street, with Scram chasing happily after her, enjoying this new game. Annie raced past the tenements with their high stoops, fat ladies in sleeveless summer dresses sitting on the steps with their stockings rolled down and paper fans in their hands. Scram followed her. Annie dodged the peddlers, ran around the Ring-O-Levio games, over a potsy board chalked on the sidewalk. Scram followed her. Annie bumped into people, sending them scattering. Scram followed her.

And the truck from the dog pound followed them both.

The dogcatcher had seen that dog before, but it had always eluded him. But today was the day. He drove to the corner ahead of Annie and the dog and put the truck into park. Then he climbed out, with a collar and leash ready, and when Annie ran past him, he braced himself for the dog.

"Gotcha! You're comin' with *me!*"

Scram let out a single high yelp of surprise as he felt the collar tighten on his neck. At the sound, Annie screeched to a halt and looked back. One glance told it all—the triumphant dogcatcher, the trapped and dejected dog. Something rose up in Annie, a feeling of protectiveness, and a feeling she'd never experienced before—possessiveness. Apart from the locket and the red sweater, what had she ever had to possess?

"Hey, mister! That's my dog!" she yelled, running back to the pound truck, and arriving nearly out of breath.

Scram wagged his tail happily at the sight of her. But the dogcatcher uttered a scornful laugh and began to drag Scram to the back door of the truck.

"Yeah? Where's his license?" he demanded skeptically. "Where's his leash? He's no more your dog than I am your father."

Annie gave him a startled glance, but he didn't have red hair.

"I left his license at home," she pleaded. "By mistake. Honest. Please don't take him to the pound. Please . . ." Now her eyes filled convincingly with tears. "My father's blind. The dog leads him to work. If he can't get to work we're gonna all of us starve. Sir, I beg you—"

"And what's his name?" *I've heard some pretty tall stories in my day,* he thought, *but this tale is taller than that new-fangled Empire State Building.*

"My father's name?" asked Annie innocently, stalling for time.

"The dog's name," said the dogcatcher pointedly.

"The dog's name?" Annie's voice rose to a squeak. She was thinking fast now, fast and furious. "His name. Uh . . . you want his name, right? Uh . . ." She looked hard at the dog, but he offered no clue. Unless . . . under the mats and the fleas and the dirt, his coat was sort of red, sort of brown . . . "His name's Sandy." *I like that,* she thought. "Right, Sandy."

By no means was the dogcatcher convinced. "Call him."

"Call him?" Annie looked panic-stricken.

The pound man loosened the rope, but didn't remove the collar. "Go over there and call him." He pointed across the street.

Oh, boy, thought Annie. *Oh, boy, oh, boy, oh, boy.* "You mean by his name?" she gulped.

"By his name," the man nodded. He was enjoying the girl's obvious discomfort. *This'll teach her, the little smarty-pants.*

Annie squared her shoulders and crossed the street. She turned and faced the dog. "Sandy!" she called. "Come here, Sandy."

Scram cocked an ear. *Is that me? Is she calling me?*

What is she doing way over there? He was confused and exhausted. The streets were crowded with people, throngs of noisy voices. Traffic was passing between him and Annie, and Scram had always been afraid of traffic, and quite rightly, too. His deepest instincts were drawing him toward Annie, but his hard-won street smarts were warning him to stay put and keep a low profile.

"Sandy! Sandy! Sandy!" shouted Annie, without hope.

By now the street had become aware that a little drama was being enacted here, with a cast of three. It looked like fun, and several showoffs decided to get in on the act.

"Here, Rover!" called a hot-dog man, laughing loudly.

"Rin Tin Tin!" cackled a toothless old newspaper vendor. "Come to mama, Rin Tin Tin!"

Scram sat up and looked from one calling face to another, now completely bewildered. Everybody seemed to be calling him, which was a novelty in itself. But everybody was calling him by a different name, which threw him further into confusion.

Above all the tooting of horns, banging and rattling of trolley cars, shouting of voices, Scram could hear one voice, one dear voice, raised in a last despairing shout. "Saaaan-deee." He stood up, fell down, got to his feet again, and trotted across the street, through the crowds and up to Annie's side, becoming in that instant Sandy forever. Jumping up, he put his paws on her shoulders, giving her face another moist lick.

This time, Annie didn't turn her face away. "Good old Sandy," she told him as she became his, just as he was already hers.

The dogcatcher came up and grudgingly took the collar off Sandy. "Well, you got yourself a dog, kid. Now go home and get him a collar and a leash."

"Yes, *sir!*" She flashed him a huge, freckled grin and the two of them ran off, Annie in the lead, Sandy hobbling gamely after her.

"Gotcha!" Out of nowhere, Officer McVie caught Annie by the collar and brought her up short. He knew who she was now, a runaway orphan, and a call to headquarters had confirmed it. The Hudson Street Home for Girls had reported her missing, red sweater, red hair, and all, only it didn't say anything about a flea-bitten mutt of a dog. "You're comin' with me."

Annie struggled, but the cop was too strong for her. Sandy launched a feeble attack, and got a boot in the chops for his pains. Leading her painfully by the scruff of the neck, the policeman marched her step by step back downtown to Hudson Street. Her moment of freedom had been brief, bittersweet, and too soon over. Now it was the orphanage for her, and another whipping.

Leapin' lizards!

CHAPTER THREE

With a sinking heart, Annie saw the grim yellow brick façade of the orphanage looming up ahead of her. Even Sandy, trotting along behind, seemed intimidated by the institution's menacing aspect, and he hung back, whining a little. The officer pulled the doorbell with a flourish; it was the old-fashioned kind on a chain. Miss Hannigan, large as life and twice as ugly, opened the door. Her face brightened when she saw the grinning face of the policeman, then darkened as she caught a glimpse of Annie.

Annie gulped in fear, and tried a friendly little smile and a wave, without success.

"Look what I found under a rock, Miss Hannigan," crowed McVie.

"Annie!" Miss Hannigan reeled back in fake happiness. "My poor little peach fuzz," she crooned. "Are you all right?" I was worried sick." She cut her eyes at the beefy cop, to see how motherly warmth went down with him. Like vanilla ice cream. "I knew you would be," and the cop edged closer. "Big-hearted woman like you."

Quick as juice through a goose, Miss Hannigan shoved Annie into the orphanage, and turned her full attention to this person in pants. He was exactly her type—"How can I ever thank you enough?" Her eyes popped suggestively, revealing tiny little red veins in the whites.

But the policeman wasn't turned off. The smell of gin excited him, promising other, more forbidden, treats. "I bet we can figure out something, if we put our heads together." Like an old fire horse responding to the fire bell, Miss Hannigan lifted up her head and whinnied in anticipation. McVie snaked one arm around her waist, and brought his face closer to hers.

"Kissy, kissy, kissy!" came from the windows above. Pepper's voice. McVie snatched his hand away as though it were on fire, and took a leap backward. The orphanage windows were filled with spying little girls, all of them grinning and sticking out their tongues.

Her dream of love evaporated, Miss Hannigan became strident. "Kill! Kill! Kill!" she shrieked, and rushed inside to wreak vengeance as the policeman stormed off.

Nobody noticed Annie's hands at the basement window, pulling it open. Nobody noticed the nondescript dog of no special color who leaped inside.

After her whipping, Annie was sent to bed without any supper. That made two bowls of mush she'd missed today; Annie would not have supposed that she'd ever be using the words "miss" and "mush" in the same sentence. But food was food, and her empty belly growled in protest. She waited for hours until the house was dark and quiet, then crept down to the kitchen on what was probably a hopeless errand. Miss Hannigan was not the kind of person who left food out for orphans to help themselves to. The shelves and cupboards were bare, and the icebox held only a block of ice. But Annie, with cunning and patience, managed to jimmy the lock on the larder, and found a half-loaf of bread.

She didn't dare take all of it. If it were missed, every orphan in the place would be punished for theft—all sixty of them—and Annie didn't want to be the cause of that. She took only enough to settle the worst pangs of her hunger. After all, when you've been hungry for ten years in a row, you kind of get used to it. Then, remembering Sandy, she carved off another piece, laid the loaf carefully back on the shelf, and replaced the lock on the larder door. Making her way to the basement slowly, not daring to turn on a light, she whispered softly into the darkness, "Sandy? Sandy, are you there?"

A happy wet lick on her cheek told her that Sandy was indeed there. She sank to the cold stone floor beside him, and wrapped her arms around his neck. *Tomorrow I give you a bath; that's a promise,* she said into his ear. Then she divided the bread between them, giving Sandy the slightly larger slice, and they shared their first meal together. When Sandy laid his head on his paws and went to

28

sleep, Annie climbed the steps to her third-floor dormitory without a sound.

All orphans over the age of eight had to work in the sweatshop, or, as Miss Hannigan put it, "The Sewing Salon." They took it in turns, and the next morning it was the turn of Annie's dorm. Molly, although only six, was allowed to stay with them, and she kept herself useful by picking up pins. Miss Hannigan kept a careful count of the pins, and heaven help the orphan who lost one.

Once they were set up for the morning's work, and Miss Hannigan had retreated to her quarters to check on the gin-filled bathtub, Annie put her fingers to her lips, and went down to the basement to fetch up Sandy. She enjoyed the gasp that went up from her audience when they saw the dog, the first dog that ever penetrated these ancient walls.

"Oh, my goodness, oh, my goodness," squeaked Tessie predictably.

"He smells," Pepper stated flatly.

"His eyes are pretty," Kate put in softly.

"What's his name, Annie?" Molly asked breathlessly, her eyes enormous with excitement.

"Guess," teased Annie with a grin.

"Fifi?" Molly's face lit up.

Duffy howled with laughter. "Fifi! What a name for a mutt like that!"

"How about Champion?" asked Kate.

"What's *he* champion of?" demanded Pepper in scorn.

"We could call him Tiger," suggested July.

Now it was July that Duffy and Pepper were hooting at.

"Tiger!" A toothless, scaredy-cat kind of a tiger!"

Through it all, Sandy sat happily, his tail thumping the floor, his eyes sparkling, giving impartial wet licks to any young face that came near his tongue.

"I got it! Rover! Rover's a good name for him," yelled Duffy.

But Annie was shaking her head. "Nope. All of you are wrong. His name's Sandy."

"Sandy. Right, I like that. Sandy, yup, that's a good name." The little girls crowded around the dog, patting him, giving him hugs, ignoring his fleas and his odor.

Here was something to love at last, and they were determined to love him, scruffy as he was, no matter how smelly.

A sudden footfall outside the sweatshop door sent the girls scrambling back to their machines. Sandy ran to hide under Annie's machine, and she draped a bedspread over the machine and down to the floor to cover him, just as the door was thrown open and Miss Hannigan stormed in.

"We love you, Miss Hannigan," chorused the girls.

Annie spun the wheel on her sewing machine and began to work the foot pedal diligently. She didn't notice there was no thread on the bobbin, but stitched away furiously. After a moment, she looked up, all innocent surprise, to see Miss Hannigan standing over her, eyes flashing with rage, foot tapping impatiently.

"Uh, I love you Miss Hannigan?" Annie took a shot at it, but with little expectation of success.

"You're going to the cellar, Annie." Miss Hannigan's voice was cold and deadly. Gasps of horror rose around her. The cellar was the most feared punishment of all, equivalent to solitary confinement for prisoners. It was dark down there, and cold and creepy, and things moved in the shadows. Slimy things, with eyes that glowed red in the dark. There were spiders in the cellar, and maybe even snakes. The basement was okay, because it had windows, but the cellar below it was a chamber of horrors.

"And *this*"—Miss Hannigan reached under Annie's machine and grabbed Sandy by the tail, pulling him out— "*this* goes to the sausage factory!" With savage glee, she saw Annie's face grow so white that the freckles stood out in relief, and her blue eyes filled with tears. It was a great day for the Hannigans when Annie could be made to cry.

Dragging Annie by one ear and Sandy by the other, she marched them toward the door, intending to lock them both in the cellar until the pound could come for Sandy. A ring at the doorbell made her hesitate, then she marched on. Whoever it was could wait.

But whoever it was at the door didn't feel much like waiting, because the bell rang again, longer and harder this time.

Muttering a curse, Miss Hannigan opened her office door and pushed the guilty pair inside, thrusting them into the supply closet. "Wait here, and don't you stir a muscle!

Don't you budge an inch!" she hissed at them. "I'll be back for you two in a minute."

All the way over from upper Fifth Avenue to the Hudson Street Home for Girls, Grace Farrell had wondered if she were doing the right thing. After all, he'd said an orphan. He hadn't been specific about a boy, just an orphan. His very words. But Miss Farrell knew he'd meant a boy orphan. She was taking an awful chance, wasn't she? And she had no idea what she would find when she got there.

First, she pictured a stern matron, her hair pulled back from her face and knotted into a tight, forbidding bun from which not one hair would ever be permitted to escape. Her image was of a tall, heavy woman in an institutional uniform, starched and pressed, perhaps with a bit of jet at the high neck of her shirtwaist as her only ornament. A stern woman, but fair. The children would be painfully neat and orderly, their uniforms dull and depressing, unsuited to childish faces and forms. Maybe their hair would be cut very short, like their fingernails.

But Grace Farrell was essentially of an optimistic turn of mind, and she turned at once to another mental picture. That of a sweet-faced Mother Superior type, with apple cheeks and kindly eyes. Her voice would be gentle whether in praise or mild admonishment, and the girls would be demure, their eyes cast down, their hands folded in obedience. Love would be the ruler here, and Miss Farrell much preferred this picture. But she was prepared to encounter the other.

What she wasn't prepared to encounter was the woman who opened the door and stuck out her angry face. Miss Farrell gave a small gasp of surprise. This woman was so . . . so . . . she searched briefly for a word, but her vocabulary for the likes of Miss Hannigan was severely limited. So *theatrical*.

She saw a tall, skinny woman teetering on high heels. Her red curls were dyed a garish color and evidently uncombed, because bits of padding could be seen sticking out, the padding that was known as "rats" and that made sparse hair look thicker. She was wearing much too much makeup. Her cheeks were rouged in round red circles like a clown's; like a clown's, too, was the absurdly heavy eye makeup and the false eyelashes. And she was a walking display rack of junk jewelry. Bangles of wood and plastic decked both her long thin arms, strings of cheap glass beads were wound around her stringy throat and cascaded down her flat chest, while a pair of long glittery earrings dangled against her cheekbones. She might not have been such a homely woman in a decent outfit, but what she was wearing made her appear like some grotesque caricature of a woman. A Hallowe'en apparition. *All she needs is a broom,* thought Grace Farrell, but she checked herself, because she was not by nature an unkind person.

"Miss Hannigan?" she asked politely.

"That's me. Who're you?" demanded the apparition.

"Miss Hannigan, I'm Grace Farrell. The New York Board of Orphans . . ."

Before she could finish her sentence, the apparition's eyes snapped open wide, and a look of terror crossed her clownish face. "W—wait . . . I have an explanation," she stammered, pulling the startled Grace Farrell out of the doorway and into the entrance hall. Miss Hannigan tugged at her nervously, while she kept talking, her free hand making anxious circular gestures in the air.

"She bribed Mr. Bundles to take her out in a laundry basket," Miss Hannigan was chattering. "I know I should have called Mr. Donatelli, but the truth of the matter is I just saw red, and called the cops. But she's back, now. So all's well that ends well, right? Right. I knew you'd agree. No harm, no foul, my little scissor legs?"

What on earth is this woman babbling about? "I'm sorry, Miss Hannigan, but what are you talking about?"

At once, the wide-open eyes narrowed into slits of suspicion, as Miss Hannigan darted into her office, with Miss Farrell following, and slammed the door shut.

"Hold it, sister. You're peddling beauty products, right? I don't need no beauty products, so you can just pedal right on out of here."

Calmly, Miss Farrell dusted off a wooden chair and sat down primly, crossing her ankles and folding her gloves neatly over her black leather purse. "Miss Hannigan, I'm the private secretary to Oliver Warbucks," she announced quietly.

The eyes snapped open again, and this time the mouth fell open to match, leaving Miss Hannigan looking like a refugee from an aquarium.

"Oliver Warbucks the millionaire?" squeaked Miss Hannigan.

"No, Oliver Warbucks the billionaire."

"The Oliver Warbucks that has more do-re-mi than all the Rockefellers put together?" The voice rose so high it almost disappeared entirely. Miss Farrell repressed the urge to laugh out loud. Although the Warbucks name always evoked the same reaction, it never failed to amuse her. Enormous fortunes seemed to impress people far more than enormous virtue or enormous wisdom.

"I don't think there's more than one," she responded quietly, a smile tugging at the corners of her mouth.

"Holy Hannah," breathed Miss Hannigan reverently, slumping back into her chair. Then she sat up and looked Miss Farrell over sharply, to see what this woman had that could induce a millionaire . . . correction, billionaire . . . to appoint her his private secretary. Darned if she could see it. Grace Farrell was wearing the worst outfit Miss Hannigan had ever seen. It was a business suit, cut of gray flannel menswear, perfectly plain, and worn with a white bow blouse that was probably silk, but without flowers printed on it, Miss Hannigan couldn't tell for sure. Her legs were encased in ordinary silk stockings, no clocks or rhinestones, and her feet were wearing a pair of narrow leather shoes with sensible heels. Aside from a gold lapel watch—with no rubies or sapphires in it, Miss Hannigan noted—the woman wore no jewelry at all, not even a ring or earrings or necklaces or bangle bracelets. Didn't Mr. Warbucks pay her a decent salary? What was she spending her money on?

And she was a young woman, too, somewhere between twenty-seven and thirty, and she might have been pretty if she curled her hair instead of wearing it rolled back so plain, and slapped on some lipstick, rouge, and mascara. Well, it was true she looked efficient, and probably that's what suited Warbucks best, but what man would want to look at efficiency after six-o'clock quitting time?

Aware of Miss Hannigan's scrutiny, Miss Farrell sat quiet for a moment. Her own thoughts were racing. Outside, while Miss Hannigan had been babbling on nervously, Miss Farrell had taken a quick look at her surroundings, and what she'd seen had appalled her. The children looked underfed and overworked; she had glimpsed the laundry room, with little girls straining over huge washboards and steaming tubs. Somewhere she could hear the hum of many sewing machines all working at once. Were these girls supposed to be working like this? Weren't they supposed to be in classes? Why were they so pale? Were there no outside exercise facilities for them? No sports or games? No romps through the park? And why were they so ragged? Weren't new clothes issued to them on a regular basis, or at least when they outgrew the old? How ironic that a place like this should be called an "asylum," when the word meant haven, a place of refuge.

She had expected nothing like this, and she was having second thoughts about her errand here. It was intended as a kindness, of course, but what if it turned out to be a cruelty instead? Was it fair to remove a child from these ghastly surroundings—and never had she seen an institution so drab, so depressing—only to throw the child right back again, and make her more miserable than before? Would it not be kinder to leave the child here, before giving her only a taste of what she was missing in life?

If the choice were hers, Grace Farrell would get up right now and leave. But it wasn't hers; she was here on instructions from Mr. Warbucks, and it was her job to carry those instructions out.

"Mr. Warbucks wants to invite an orphan to spend a week with him in his home," she said clearly. "I'm here to select one."

Annie, in Miss Hannigan's supply closet, had been listening hard to every word. She'd opened the closet door a fraction of an inch, and had been looking at Grace Farrell. My, that was the prettiest lady she'd ever seen, prettier than any of them in the Sunday rotogravures. So elegantly dressed, with such a shining, clean face, and such beautiful, kind gray eyes. And her hair was rolled away from her face and pinned neatly back, just like Annie's own mother in the Dream. Annie bet this lady didn't get drunk and call helpless orphans pig droppings. She pushed the closet door open a little and flashed Miss Farrell her very brightest freckle-faced grin, turning the volume on her charm control way, way up.

"Wonderful," Miss Hannigan was saying without enthusiasm, having barely recovered from the shock of Miss Farrell's announcement. "What sort of orphan did he have in mind?" She saw Miss Farrell's eyes widen slightly as she caught a glimpse of Annie grinning from the closet, and she slammed the door hard, nearly catching Annie's nose in it.

"Well . . ." Miss Farrell hesitated, captured by the image of the little girl's smiling face. "Friendly and intelligent . . ."

The closet door opened again, and Annie's face appeared, looking friendly and intelligent with all its might.

"M-I-Double-S-I-Double-S-I-Double-P-I," she chanted, proving her smarts.

Hannigan turned, snarling, and shoved her back into the closet again, slamming the door extra hard. "You're asking for it, my little prune pit."

"And happy," continued Miss Farrell, her amused eyes on the closet door. The door opened silently and Annie mimed being happy, clutching at her ribs and mouthing laughter.

"The trials of a working woman," sighed Miss Hannigan with an elaborate show of put-upon patience.

"I'm in somewhat of a hurry, Miss Hannigan," Miss Farrell replied with a frosty smile.

"Of course," snapped Miss Hannigan, dragging a manila file folder toward her officiously. "How old?"

"Oh, the age doesn't matter. Seven or eight . . ."

The closet door opened a fraction of an inch and Annie's little hand signaled frantically.

"Or nine . . ."

Another frantic signal.

"Or ten?"

The hand gave a little "on-the-button" wave.

"Yes, ten, I think," said Grace Farrell.

The little hand appeared again, this time tugging at a curly lock of carrot hair. Miss Farrell suppressed a grin; she was enjoying this game, enjoying, too, the audacity and spunk of this youngster. The child had formed an alliance with her against Miss Hannigan, and in the most ingenious way.

"Oh, I almost forgot. Mr. Warbucks prefers redheaded children."

Miss Hannigan whipped around suspiciously, but the closet door presented the most bland and innocent aspect a closed door could offer. "A ten-year-old redhead?" she retorted briskly. "Nope. Sorry. Don't have one."

Ta-da! The closet door was flung open wide, and Annie stepped out, to the imaginary flourish of invisible trumpets. "What about *this* child?" asked Miss Farrell, standing up.

"Annie?" shrieked Miss Hannigan, aghast. "Oh, no, you wouldn't want Annie. She's—" she searched for an epithet dreadful enough to scare Miss Farrell off, "she's an imp."

Grace Farrell uttered a short laugh, and took the child by the hand. "Oh, fiddle-faddle. Annie, would you like to spend a week at Mr. Warbucks' house?"

The electric lights of Times Square would have been pale candles to Annie's joyous face. "Oh, boy! I would love to! I would really, really love to!" She fairly danced in excitement.

"Hold it!" barked Miss Hannigan, who was really furious now. "You can have any orphan in the orphanage, except Annie."

"Why?" demanded Grace Farrell hotly.

Miss Hannigan snatched the child away from the younger woman and thrust her behind her office chair. Her words came out through clenched teeth, as though every one was being bitten off and spat out. "Because she's got it coming to her, and I don't mean a week in the lap of luxury. This brat needs to learn her place."

"Her place?" Miss Farrell's eyebrows rose toward her hat brim.

"I rent out my older girls as domestics. Annie's entirely too cheeky."

"Mr. Warbucks likes cheeky orphans." Heaven forgive me for that lie.

"Tough," spat Miss Hannigan, and it was obvious to Grace that the other woman didn't intend to yield an

inch. And a curious stubbornness was creeping over Miss
Farrell herself, taking her rather by surprise, for she con-
sidered herself to be a businesslike and practical young
woman. Was it something special about this freckle-faced
little girl, or was it just the Irish in Farrell? She wasn't
sure. But she discovered that she was just as determined
to take this child as Miss Hannigan was to prevent her
from going. And she surprised herself even further by her
next tactic. She didn't think she had it in her.

"I assume your resistance has something to do with Mr.
Donatelli and the board of orphans—" she began icily.

"Don't assume nothing, sweetheart," hissed Miss Hannigan.

"Mr. Warbucks and Mr. Donatelli are like this," she
continued, holding up her right hand with the two first
fingers crossed.

She's lying, thought Hannigan. *She's bluffing.* She gave
an elaborate yawn of boredom, then buffed her fingernails
on her blouse and studied them carefully. "Is that a fact,"
she said. It was not a question.

"Yes, that's a fact," went on Grace Farrell, her face
betraying nothing. "And it's a further fact that Mr. Donatelli was at the house just last week saying how many
people he had lined up for your job." And she, too,
studied her hands, as she pulled her gloves on carefully,
finger by finger.

She's bluffing, Miss Hannigan told herself again, but
with far less conviction. Yet it was far from impossible,
very far. "Is that a fact?" And this time it was a question.

"Awful time to be unemployed," Miss Farrell com-
mented.

"Just terrible," agreed Miss Hannigan.

A long moment passed between them, during which
time Grace Farrell sent up a little prayer of thanks that
Miss Hannigan had babbled to her of a Mr. Donatelli,
whoever he was, and a little prayer without words, for
Annie.

At last, without a word, Miss Hannigan shoved Annie
roughly at Miss Farrell. She couldn't take the chance, not
with unemployment figures so high. Besides, the kid would
be back in a week, and would she get it then! Miss Hanni-

gan would devote the entire week to devising new and fiendish punishments. *I deserve a treat,* she told herself.

"Leapin' lizards!" yelled Annie ecstatically, and Grace Farrell allowed herself a broad smile.

"Come along, dear. Mr. Warbucks' limousine is waiting." She was rather pleased with herself at the way she'd handled that, and could wish that Mr. Warbucks had been there to see it. Of course, if Oliver Warbucks *had* been present, nothing would have had to be handled. He was accustomed to commanding immediate obedience, and receiving it.

But Annie was hanging back now, her face clouded, her blue eyes anxious.

"My dog," she said simply.

Miss Farrell's gray eyes widened. "Your what?" she gasped, but Annie was already pulling open the supply closet door, and leading out Sandy. He was the worst-looking, scruffiest, dirtiest, least-prepossessing mongrel Miss Farrell had encountered in all her twenty-eight years, but before she could open her mouth to protest, Sandy bounded over to her.

"He's really nice, really quiet, really, really good," Annie was assuring her. "He never jumps up on people."

As if on cue, Sandy jumped up on Grace, his muddy paws on her custom-tailored suit, his hot breath on her face and . . . oh, no . . . gave her a really wet, really slobbering kiss, pushing her hat nearly off.

She took a few steps backward, shaking her head, and tried to get her breath back. "I'm afraid not, Annie. He's very sweet, but Mr. Warbucks—"

"Then I'm not coming," said Annie, not defiantly, but with sad determination.

Both women turned to her in astonishment, but Annie met their gaze firmly. They could see that this was very hard for her, for her expressive face had grown quite pale, and her lips were trembling.

Miss Hannigan recovered first. "Mr. Warbucks wouldn't rather have a good-looking lady?" she wheedled, patting at her ratty hair. "I got a week coming."

Annie took a step forward and grabbed Grace Farrell by the hand. "She's going to send him to the sausage factory," she pleaded. "She said so herself."

Grace gasped and turned a face of outrage upon Miss Hannigan, who defended herself sullenly. "I'm not zoned for dogs."

"We'll take the dog," decided Miss Farrell. *Heaven help me, what am I doing? Mr. Warbucks will have my hide.*

Annie's face reflected her happiness. "Oh, boy!" she exulted.

As they walked toward the front door, Miss Farrell was feeling dazed and even a little helpless. What had she done? Oliver Warbucks had sent her to fetch an orphan boy of good manners and a retiring disposition, and no dog. And here she was coming back with a feisty, rambunctious redheaded girl and a dog of uncertain parentage whose enthusiasm for life and noisy way of showing it matched the girl's own. And to top it off, the dog smelled to high heaven and had fleas! How unlike her usual efficiency; what *would* Mr. Warbucks say?

And yet, as she led the way to the twenty-five-foot-long limousine (*Holy Hannah!* wailed Miss Hannigan silently. *A Town Car!*) with the license plate NY-1, a license plate that by tradition belonged to the governor of New York until Mr. Warbucks decided he wanted it, Grace Farrell felt that there was nothing she wanted to change. She felt a pull toward this bright little girl with the carroty mop, as though they'd known each other for years, in a dream perhaps. She felt that this was the child she had come to get, pure and simple. Yes, is was only for a week, and back Annie would have to go, into Miss Hannigan's vicious clutches. But a week, well spent, could be a very long time. Who knows what could happen in a week?

Annie didn't take the time to examine the luxurious limousine and the strange-looking Oriental, dressed all in black, at the wheel, she was so eager to get started. She couldn't believe her luck. This day had been so full already, with more to come. Sandy danced into the Town Car as to the manor born, and Annie was about to follow, when she heard a commotion above.

The orphans were crowded at the windows, waving and yelling, and Molly, predictably, was in tears.

"Don't go, Annie!" she wailed, heart-broken.

Annie grinned and waved. A week wasn't so long. "I'll be back!" she promised. "I'll bring everybody presents!"

Then, minding her manners, she carefully wiped her feet, cleaning each shoe on the back of her other leg before she stepped into the Town Car. She could smell the leather and the lovely clean scent of the beeswax that kept the leather polished. The interior was of Honduras mahogany, with solid silver fittings; there were curtains at the windows and fresh roses in little silver-and-crystal vases on the car's walls. Annie looked about her in astonishment, then sank happily back on the leather cushions as the car pulled silently away from the curb and picked up speed.

This has been the very best day of my life, she told herself as they headed uptown. *And it's not over yet.*

This is the worst day of my life, growled Miss Hannigan to herself as she watched the Town Car speed off. *But I'll get even. That miserable troublemaker, that rotten kid, will be the sorriest orphan in the universe when I get my hands on her again.*

CHAPTER FOUR

You've been to Buckingham Palace, haven't you? I know you have, because the Queen asked for you by name the last time I had tea there. And you've been to Louis the Sun King's glorious palace at Versailles, and to the Metropolitan Museum of Art in New York, and to the Vatican in Rome. But Annie had never been to any of these places, so she was totally unprepared for Oliver Warbucks' mansion on upper Fifth Avenue.

First of all, you entered through a tall pair of iron gates, always kept locked, which led to a long, circular driveway. The Asp, who was driving the Town Car, took a mysterious magnetic device out of his uniform pocket and the gates opened as if by magic. The Town Car slid purring up the driveway and stopped without a bump or quiver outside the broad steps and the huge carved-oak doors.

Annie peeked out of the window. A stone and marble edifice four stories high filled two city blocks. It was a villa in the Italian Renaissance style, designed by Stanford White. The windows were topped by arched pediments; there were elaborately carved acanthus ornaments at the house corners. The house boasted a copper roof, which gleamed in the sunlight. Two massive lions of stone guarded the entrance, paws raised in silent warning. It was by far the largest building Annie had ever seen, and she was thrilled at its majesty.

"Are we going on a train? Is this a train station?" she asked Miss Farrell excitedly.

Grace Farrell smiled down at her and shook her head. "No, dear, this is Mr. Warbucks' house."

"Leapin' lizards!" breathed Annie. She tumbled out of the car after Miss Farrell, and Sandy followed clumsily, his paws sliding on the marble steps.

The thick oak doors opened suddenly, and Annie froze on the spot, her mouth open in astonishment. Standing in the doorway, almost filling it, was the tallest man Annie had ever seen. He was so tall he made the stone lions look like kittens beside him. His skin was very dark, almost black, and he wore a strange uniform, with golden epaulets on the shoulders of a long, white, form-fitting tunic. Golden chains were looped around his neck and over his chest, gold flashed on his dark fingers. On his head, the nine-foot-tall giant wore a huge turban made of a rare silk cloth shot with threads of gold, and wound round and round and round until the many yards of it had been tucked neatly into the knotted headdress. From the center of the turban, topped by an egret feather, flashed a pigeon's-blood ruby, the rarest in all India, and it caught the sunlight and turned into a heart of fiery flame. The man's lips parted in what he believed to be a smile, but to Annie it was a grin of such terror-inducing menace that she squeaked in fear and ran to hide behind Grace Farrell's skirts. Annie wasn't afraid of much, but she'd never encountered anything like this man before. Why, his black polished boots were almost large enough for her to hide in!

Sandy, sensing Annie's fear and scared to death of this man-mountain himself, broke into hysterical barking.

In an instant, everything was noise and confusion— Annie hiding and near tears, Sandy almost hoarse with barking. Grace was unable to hear herself think. She glared at the Asp, who, with Oriental calm and detachment, remained seated behind the wheel of the Town Car.

"You're a big help," she told him in an exasperated tone, trying to be heard over the barking.

The Asp shrugged slightly. "I have to put the car in the garage," he said mildly, but Grace had the sneaking feeling he was enjoying all this in his silent way.

She reached around her and pulled the quaking Annie out of hiding. "Annie, this is Punjab," she said, indicating the giant in the Indian officer's uniform. "Punjab and the Asp are Mr. Warbucks' bodyguards. There's nothing to be afraid of."

Punjab raised his hands in the air and made a couple of mysterious passes. At once, Sandy stopped barking, walked up the stairs in a straight line, and stopped at Punjab's feet. There he lay down on his back, all four feet in the air, and a doggy smile on his face.

Annie's fear evaporated. Wow, what a trick! Could he teach her that? She ran up the steps, her right hand extended for a shake.

"I'm Annie," she grinned. "Boy, I wouldn't want to come across you in a dark alley."

Punjab leaned down solemnly and took the little girl's hand into his large black one, where it disappeared entirely. A current of energy passed between them; both felt it, as though electricity had forged them together. He looked deeply into her eyes.

Now they passed into the entrance hallway, where Annie gasped again. Huge and mirrored, with a massive chandelier of scintillating crystal drops reflecting from the marble floors, the entrance hall alone was fifty feet long and forty wide. Heavy paintings hung on the walls between the elaborately carved mirror frames, and below them, on console tables of gilded wood, stood bronze statues, marble busts and gigantic bouquets of hothouse blooms in rare Ming vases. On an easel stood a framed Rembrandt, looking almost lost in the vastness of the space around it. Tall curio cabinets held priceless T'ang horses of jade and other precious stones, exquisite examples of Greek pottery from the fifth century B.C., and tiny porphyry vases of Egypt's Middle Kingdom. At the end of the vast hallway, a graceful staircase of marble curved upward to the higher floors.

"Wow!" Annie breathed, unable to say more. An army of servants was mopping, dusting, polishing, and scrubbing the already gleaming surfaces. One man in a footman's uniform was standing on tiptoe on the highest rung of a fourteen-foot ladder, dusting the moldings with an ostrich-feather duster on a long pole. Another, with a large can of marble cleaner, was rubbing a coat of it into the staircase. Two other footmen, with lamb's-wool buffers strapped to their feet, were skating down the hallway, adding an extra gloss to the highly polished and very slick floor. Standing at a sideboard, the head butler, Drake, was putting the finishing touches on an elaborate Georgian silver tea service, making certain that no stain of tarnish, no matter how tiny, marred the flawless surface of the silver.

Sandy, bounding with doggy enthusiasm into the entry, slipped and skidded on the polished floor. As his paws went out from under him, he scrabbled desperately in the air, found his footing, lost it again, and went skidding and skittering all the long way down the hallway, to fetch up at the disdainful feet of Drake, the head butler.

Drake inclined his aristocratic head only enough to look down his nose at his formerly glistening black shoes, now covered by a scruffy and unpleasant-smelling canine of no discernible ancestry and certainly of no breeding. Drake uttered a disapproving sneeze.

"I take it you've been to the zoo, Miss Farrell?"

"Not recently, Drake." Miss Farrell took on an air of command as she marched down the endless foyer with Drake at her side. She fired a string of questions at him.

"Has the organ been tuned, the pool heated, the floors waxed . . . well, yes"—with an amused glance at Sandy, who was living proof the floor was waxed as he skidded after Annie and Grace Farrell—"is the tennis court net up, the French doors fixed, the elevator oiled, the typewriter repaired, the second teletype installed, and the photographer here?"

It was only then, as the last question brought them to a baronial chair outside the drawing room, in which a little man with a belted raincoat and a slouch-brim fedora sat clutching a huge Speed Graphic with flashbulb attachments, that Drake was able to slip in an edgewise word.

"Yes, Miss Farrell," and he sneezed again, casting a venomous glare at Sandy.

"Allergic to dogs, Drake?"

"No," said the butler, with his nose as far into the air as he could send it, "filth."

Grace Farrell turned to see Mrs. Pugh, the cook, bustling up, tying on a clean apron.

"Is dinner under way, Mrs. Pugh?"

"Yes, miss," and the plump cook beamed all over her rosy face. "I'm preparing his favorite. Texas grapefruit, Virginia ham, Idaho potatoes, Wisconsin cheese, Washington apples, and baked Alaska."

"Good. Now, everybody listen, please. I have an announcement to make that concerns you all."

The staff stopped waxing, polishing, dusting, scrubbing, scouring, and tidying and turned its full attention to Miss Farrell. She, in turn, looked around for Annie, who was standing behind her, half hidden, with her china-blue eyes as large and as round as saucers with sheer astonishment at all this undreamt-of grandeur.

"This is Annie. She'll be staying with us for a week."

The staff came crowding around to have a look, and Annie found herself in the thick of black uniforms and white aprons, polished shoes and boots and curious faces.

"Miss." Were they bowing to *her*, to a little orphan named Annie? Leapin' lizards!

"And her dog Sandy," said Miss Farrell graciously.

"Who'll be staying with *me*," put in Annie, to a general outbreak of laughter from everybody but Drake.

The prettiest of the three chambermaids, Annette, took a step forward. "May I take your sweater, miss?"

Annie clutched at her precious red sweater, which was half of everything she owned. "Will I get it back?"

"Lord love you, yes, miss."

Reluctantly, Annie took it off and handed it over, but kept an anxious eye on it for a minute or two.

"Now, Annie," said Grace Farrell, "what would you like to do first?"

Annie looked around carefully, thinking hard. Then she made up her mind. "The windows," she said decisively. "Then the floors." She began rolling up the sleeves of her shabby smock. "That way, if I drip—"

The explosion of hilarity interrupted and surprised her. Everybody—with the natural exception of Drake—was laughing fit to bust, the footmen guffawing, the maids giggling, Mrs. Pugh holding her ample sides. Even Grace Farrell was laughing as she bent to give the child a quick hug.

"Oh, Annie, you won't have to do any cleaning while you're here."

Annie was totally bewildered now. "I won't? How'm I going to earn my keep?" she asked, her tiny brow puckered with doubt.

Grace Farrell was smiling into her eyes, Grace Farrell

had taken both of Annie's hands in hers, and Annie saw again how lovely she was.

"You're our *guest*, Annie," said Miss Farrell softly. "We'll take care of you. You're to have new clothing, and Cecille will help you dress and comb your hair. There will be bubbles in your bathtub, and clean satin sheets on your bed. When you've decided what you want to eat, just let Mrs. Pugh know, and you shall have it for your next meal, whatever it is."

The saucers of Annie's eyes grew to the size of dinner plates. Could she believe her ears?

"You'll find the swimming pool downstairs," continued Miss Farrell.

"A swimming pool inside the house?" This was too good to be true. "Oh, boy!"

"You do play tennis, don't you? We have a tennis court outside. Two, actually, one grass and one clay."

Overwhelmed, Annie shook her head. "I . . . I . . . never even saw a tennis racquet," she admitted.

"Have an instructor here at noon," Grace said to Drake. "Oh, and get that Don Budge fellow, if he's available." Drake went off to the telephone at once to see if Budge was available. And he was, for after all, he wasn't going to win the Grand Slam for another five years, or the Wimbledon singles and doubles for another four.

Annie's head was whirling so she was afraid it would lift off her neck and go flying around the room. When Annette, Cecille, and Miss Farrell showed her to the room she would sleep in, she almost passed out cold! She had more space than all the orphans in the Hudson Street Home for Girls, Established 1891, had put together. A huge pink bed, with pink counterpane and matching canopy, tied back with sprigs of roses. A full-length mirror framed in gold, in which Annie could see a shabby red-headed orphan with an ear-to-ear grin on her face. Closets that she was assured would be filled with clothes; shelves that she was told would be crammed with books and toys. A bathroom, all her very own, with a thick soft rug and double-thick terry towels. Annie had never seen a terry towel before; at the orphanage, all they had were basins of tepid water, ice-cold floors, and ragged "towels" made of old flour sacks. It was all so overwhelming that she couldn't take it in at once. It was making her dizzy, and she collapsed on the thick carpeting in a heap, followed by Sandy, who melted into a canine puddle next to her, still wagging his tail furiously.

It was time for Miss Farrell to take charge, to put her famous efficiency to use. Annette she sent to the Fifth Avenue shops, De Pinna and Best and Company, to collect a suitable wardrobe for a ten-year-old child and bring it back at once. And, since Annie had no clothes to wear now anyway, why not go swimming first, then lunch? Somewhere there was a bathing suit to fit her; the undergardener had a daughter just about Annie's size. Would that do?

Would that do! Swimming! Although she had never swum before (a fact she neglected to mention to Miss Farrell), Annie took to it like a baby duck, first paddling around in imitation of Sandy, who never left her side, just in case, and later developing almost a sidestroke. Miss Farrell, watching from the side of the turquoise pool with the Roman mosaics on the floor, made a mental note to see if Eleanor Holm, the swimming star, might be persuaded to drop by and show Annie the butterfly stroke.

Most of the staff, instead of returning to their duties, hung around the swimming pool to watch Annie. They had never had—or ever expected to have—a little girl in this house. They had seen princes and prime ministers come in and go out through the big oak doors, plutocrats, philosophers, poets, pundits, and playwrights (Mr. Warbucks being quite chummy with Mr. Bernard Shaw), but Annie was a novelty, and they watched her splashing around in delight. Her enjoyment brought smiles to their faces, with the exception of Drake, to be sure, who closed his eyes in horror as Sandy spread dirt and fleas in the chlorinated water. They'd have to drain the pool.

Suddenly, what sounded like an air-raid siren went off with a head-splitting wail. All at once, the servants began rushing to the exit, jostling one another aside in their haste to get out. As they ran, they were straightening their hair anxiously, patting hair nets into place, checking the buttons on their uniform jackets, retying the bows of their aprons more neatly.

"What is it?" asked Annie fearfully, climbing out of the

47

pool. Sandy clambered out after her and shook himself mightily, spraying water everywhere.

"It's Mr. Warbucks," replied Miss Farrell, distracted. "Don't be afraid." But she herself was looking anxious, checking the seams of her stockings, smoothing down the skirt of her tailored suit. In an undertone she gave orders that Annie be taken up to her room, dressed and combed and brought right back down again. Then she herself hurried off to be at the front door when Mr. Warbucks came in. The noisy siren had signaled that his car—today he'd taken the Dusenberg, with the license plate NY-2, which used to belong to the lieutenant governor—had reached the garage. The siren was known to the staff as the Two-Minute Warning, or Oh-Oh, Here He Comes.

Because Annie had almost nothing to wear, and because her mop of red curls defied any comb, she was down in time to see the front doors open and Oliver Warbucks stride in, flanked on either side by Punjab and the Asp. A sudden shyness seized her, and she hid behind one of the great marble pillars in the hall, peeping out with curiosity at this man who held so much power over so many.

She saw a tall man of commanding presence, a man who walked with his spine as stiff as a broomstick, his head held high. It was a strange head, bald as a peeled hard-boiled egg, shaven clean every day. The jaw was strong and jutting, the mouth stubborn, yet it was a handsome face. From where she was hiding, Annie couldn't see the color of Oliver Warbucks' eyes, but she could see them glinting and she guessed—correctly—that they were the color of steel. It was a stern face, but not a mean one. Impatient, arrogant but not vain. Oliver Warbucks looked to be a man of large faults, but no little frailties. Annie decided she liked him, but she knew she was also a little afraid of him. Sandy cowered at her feet, his paws over his eyes.

Warbucks was dressed in a suit of black, with a vest that bore a heavy gold chain across his middle, from which hung various golden nuggets. A diamond stickpin glittered on his shirt. A stiff collar and a somewhat old-fashioned black bow tie completed the costume of a billionaire. Annie was to learn that this was his invariable costume, and that he had vast closets crammed with identical copies of this very suit, drawers filled with hundreds and hundreds of white stiff-collared shirts. He had no patience with valets, or choosing neckties, or matching blue shirts to brown tweeds. Oliver Warbucks knew what he liked, and when he found it, he stuck to it.

"Welcome home, sir," she could hear Grace Farrell say, as Warbucks marched to the sideboard where the silver tea service was standing ready. He took no tea, however, but accepted the brandy and the Havana cigar that she was lighting for him.

He didn't return the greeting, but asked abruptly, "Did the painting arrive?"

"They're uncrating it now, sir," said Grace quietly, indicating with a slight movement of her head where two men in coveralls were carefully lifting a painting out of an elaborately constructed wooden packing case that bore steamship labels from the S.S. *Normandie*. They turned the painting around so that it faced Warbucks.

Oliver Warbucks stared at it for a minute, scowling.

"I hate it. Send it back," he said finally. "Any messages?"

Grace Farrell had learned to keep her opinions to herself, but she could barely repress a gasp. Hate it? Hate the *Mona Lisa*, Leonardo's masterpiece, the most famous portrait in the history of art? But all she said was, "President Roosevelt called three times this morning. Said it was urgent."

Behind her pillar, Annie *did* gasp. The president of the United States! Why, Roosevelt was Annie's hero! He was going to make things better for everybody, even orphans! Annie had heard it on Miss Hannigan's radio, the last time Miss Hannigan had obliged them by passing out.

Warbucks' scowl deepened. "Everything's urgent to a Democrat," he rasped. He spoke with a slight accent, one that Annie had never heard before. "What else?"

Miss Farrell consulted her message pad. "Mr. Rockefeller, Mr. DuPont, Mr. Vanderbilt, Mr. Carnegie . . ."

"Wait!" barked Warbucks. The men lowering the painting back into the Louvre's packing crate stopped, suspended at the billionaire's command. "There's something interesting in that woman's smile. I might learn to like her. Take her upstairs and hang her in my bathroom."

They nodded immediately, and lifted *La Gioconda* back out of the case, using the utmost delicacy, for no value could be set on this painting; it was absolutely priceless, and the Louvre had parted with it only after Warbucks had rescued France's failing economy single-handed.

"Mr. Warbucks, I'd like you to meet—" began Miss Farrell, but Warbucks paid no attention. Which was just as well, because Annie was still hiding behind the pillar, trying to get up the nerve to emerge and be introduced.

Briskly, Warbucks picked up his briefcase again and headed for the stairs, issuing crisp commands over his shoulder.

"I've no time for dinner tonight, Mrs. Pugh. Send up an American cheese sandwich at midnight." The plump cook's face fell as she thought of her lovely dinner going uneaten. But she didn't dare to do more than nod her acquiescence.

"Come on, Miss Farrell, let's get started," ordered Warbucks, making an abrupt turn, and nearly falling over Annie, who had decided to come out after all, but who'd chosen the wrong moment and the wrong place. As soon as she and Warbucks collided, the photographer leaped up with his trusty Speed Graphic and snapped their picture with a brilliant and noisy pop of his flashbulb.

Between tripping over the child and having a flashbulb go off unexpectedly in his face, Warbucks was totally at a loss, a situation he found himself in almost never. He opened his mouth and let out a roar.

"Punjab."

Like a streak of black lightning, the Indian giant was across the lobby and on the photographer, pinning him against the wall with one huge hand, while the other crumpled the expensive camera as if it were so much cellophane.

"What the devil is going on here?" bellowed Warbucks.

"Forgive me, sahib. Miss Farrell said—"

Grace was talking at the same time, "This is Annie, sir, the orphan who'll be staying with us for a week."

Warbucks looked down at Annie, his brow furrowed, the corners of his mouth turning down in the scowl that was so characteristic of him. "Orphan? What are you talking about?" He pointed a finger at the shaken photographer. "Who's he?"

In her most soothing tones, Miss Farrell reminded her employer gently, "The public relations people? Your image?" Warbucks' scowl was now looking puzzled. It was obvious he had no idea what his secretary was babbling about.

"They wanted photographs of you sharing your home with an orphan, sir, don't you remember? It's just for a week, sir."

Annie held her breath, begging him silently to remember.

"Oh," said Mr. Warbucks. "Yes," said Mr. Warbucks. "Hmmm," said Mr. Warbucks. He looked a little embarrassed and uncomfortable, then he took a long, hard look at Annie.

"But this doesn't look like a boy," he told Miss Farrell. "Orphans are boys."

I was afraid this would happen, thought Grace. *Poor Annie.* "You didn't say you wanted a boy," she spoke up rather bravely. "You just said orphan. So I got a girl," she finished in a much smaller voice.

Warbucks gave her a steely stare. "I want a boy." He turned his back on them both and headed once more for the stairs, but Annie trotted by his side.

"I've got an interesting smile too, sir." She grinned up at him anxiously. "Don'tcha think maybe you could learn to like me, too, sir? Hang me in the bathroom?" She waited hopefully for a response, but he didn't even crack a smile. Oliver Warbucks' mind was elsewhere. He turned to Miss Farrell sharply.

"Why do I smell wet dog?" he demanded.

Grace winced, and opened her mouth to make some explanation, then shut it again. Seeing her predicament, Annie snapped her fingers. At once, a fearful, soaking Sandy, looking like an oversized wet mop with a hangover, crawled out from behind the pillar and slid on his belly over to Annie's feet. He still didn't trust that waxed floor.

"Because Sandy got wet in the pool, sir," said Annie.

Warbucks stared at the mutt in disbelief. That wretched object, under the same roof with his Rembrandt and his Leonardo Da Vinci? He looked across at Grace Farrell, whose cheeks were stained dull red with embarrassment. "Take them back," he commanded, his voice dripping with ice. "Now."

"Oh, sir," pleaded Grace through the lump rising in her throat. "She only got here." She felt far worse for Annie than she did for herself, although it was her own neck and her own job that were on the line here.

But Annie was stepping up bravely, Annie was forcing a smile. "That's okay, Miss Farrell. We'll be okay," she was saying. The little girl turned to Oliver Warbucks and held her right hand out. "It's been real nice meeting you, sir, anyhow. I sure do like your place . . ."

Still a little dazed from the experience of meeting an orphan of the wrong gender and a dog of the wrong everything, Mr. Warbucks finally noticed the small hand, took it faintly and shook it a little.

"Thank you, Annette, I—"

"Annie," interrupted Annie. "I've really had a swell time already. The Asp drove us here in a car the size of a train, Mr. Warbucks, and Punjab put a spell on Sandy, and we made Drake sneeze, and we saw your tennis court, and Sandy got to swim in your pool, and . . . well . . . I've had enough fun to last me for years. It's a really swell idea to have an orphan for a week, Mr. Warbucks, a really terrific idea, even if it's only for a week, and only for your image, and even if I'm not the orphan. I'm glad you're doing it."

Incredulous, Oliver Warbucks finally found his voice. "I'm glad you approve." He turned to his secretary. "Let's get to work," he said impatiently, burning to begin. Time was his most precious commodity; he already had more money than the country of India or the state of Rhode Island.

Going up the stairs, Grace said hesitantly, "Since we have so much to do, maybe I could take her back in the morning?" She snuck a look at Mr. Warbucks to see how he would take this suggestion.

But he was already opening his mail, and paying only scant attention to her words. "Whatever. Let's go!"

Annie and Grace exchanged one brief, joyous, triumphant glance. At least, Annie had been reprieved until morning. And who knows what might happen between now and morning? Why, anything! Then Grace Farrell dashed up the stairs after Oliver Warbucks, ready to put in many long hours of work.

As for Annie, although she had meant what she said to Oliver Warbucks, she was delighted for her sake that she could stay the night. Just to sleep in that wonderful bed, with the counterpane and canopy of roses, and all that room! Just to spend the rest of the day here, in this palace, to try to get every detail by heart to tell the other orphans when she went back in the morning . . . in the morning. Annie sighed, thinking of the morning, but she brightened again. She was going to make this day last, squeeze every drop of joy from it that she could.

"C'mon, Sandy! If we've got only one day, let's make the most of it."

CHAPTER FIVE

After the Town Car had turned the corner, carrying the rotten kid to her unjust reward, Miss Hannigan did what any self-respecting person with red blood in her veins would do. She went into her room, locked the door, and tied one on. Miss Hannigan was contemplating the injustices of this world, and the many and awful crosses she had to bear on the rock-strewn pathway of her life.

"Little girls," she muttered to herself, flinging herself across a bed strewn with torn stockings, dirty kimonos, and old movie magazines with Jean Harlow on their covers, "little girls, how I hate 'em. Look at me, I'm still young, I'm still beautiful [this was a favorite fantasy of Miss Hannigan's], I'd make some lucky man a wonderful wife, but why am I stuck here with sixty miserable, rotten, whiny, nasty, hateful, horrible little girls?" She moaned, and staggered off the bed to wobble to the mirror and contemplate her bleary image.

"I should be out dancing somewhere, somewhere where a tango orchestra is playing, and the night is young. I should be wearing fox furs and a diamond necklace. Not many women can carry off diamonds, but I can," she told her reflection confidingly. "I should be driving around in a *big* car, a Reo maybe, or an Olds, and going to the movies every night with a box of chocolate-covered cherries. Instead, here I am stuck playing nursemaid to sixty of the schemingest, most defiant, freshest bunch of ungrateful individuals that God ever put on this earth to torture a poor, hardworking creature like me who never harmed the hair on the head of a fly." She was in the self-pity stage now, which was usually followed by blind rage, then the blind staggers, and then she usually passed out.

"What have I ever done to deserve all these children?" moaned Miss Hannigan, taking another hefty swig from the flask. "Not that I wouldn't be a perfect mother, kind, gentle, loving, totally unselfish and giving, self-sacrificing, devoted, saintly, caring for the hideous little brats night and day with never a thought for my own comfort or convenience."

Breaking off to take another long drink from the flask, Miss Hannigan drained it to the last lethal drop. *Thish will never do. Gotta filler up again. Mish Hannigan needs her vitamins, or thoshe li'l monshters will get the better of her.* Miss Hannigan was so preoccupied that she didn't hear any sound at all from the other room, with the result that when she wandered back into her bedroom and saw a strange man and a strange woman sitting on her bed, she was so startled that she let out one loud scream and sobered up almost completely.

"Hi, sis!" said the strange man with a grin.

Miss Hannigan squinted to see him better. There *was* something vaguely familiar about that ratty little face with its pointed weasel nose, squirrel teeth, beady little eyes, and no chin. The ratty little face had grown a thin moustache since the last time Miss Hannigan had laid eyes on it, and that's what had thrown her off.

"Rooster!" she cried without pleasure as she recognized her brother. "Aren't you a sight for sore eyes, Rooster? What is this, did they let you out of jail early?"

"On account of his good behavior," simpered the woman, whom Miss Hannigan had never seen before. She was snuggled so close to Rooster Hannigan, it appeared she wanted to force her way through him to the other side.

"Sis," said he with a complacent male grin, "meet a little friend of mine, Lily St. Regis."

Miss Hannigan turned no friendly face in the young woman's direction. She saw a bleached blonde, round in all the places where Miss Hannigan was flat, wearing a tight rayon satin dress, black net stockings, and four-inch heels. Her face might have been pretty if you could see it, but it was hidden under so many layers of makeup that the features were almost indistinguishable, except for the mouth, which was painted in the form of a perfect cupid's bow.

"St. Regis," the young woman giggled. "Named for the hotel." She tightened her grasp on Rooster, as though afraid he was going to make a break for the exit.

"You couldn't find the Waldorf?" Miss Hannigan asked her brother, her voice dripping with sarcasm. She wasn't happy to see Rooster; on the contrary, he never came around unless he wanted something, and that something was invariably money. He had ways of getting it, too, ways that Miss Hannigan recalled were customarily unpleasant. There was no love lost between these two, but at least Miss Hannigan worked for part of her living. Rooster stole for all of his.

Now his arm was stealing, stealing around his sister's shoulder as he turned her attention away from his girlfriend, who was quietly rummaging through Miss Hannigan's personal possessions, helping herself to the bits and pieces she fancied. She slipped rings on her fingers, bracelets on her arms, and tucked lavalieres and strings of beads into her dress.

"Sis, this very afternoon I put me a ten on the nose of this darling horse, eight to one. Sure enough, the scumbum took off and whipped the pack." Rooster's little eyes glittered with the scam.

"Rooster, that's great. Let's celebrate," grinned Miss Hannigan, always ready for another drink.

Now Rooster's voice dropped an octave, and he gave his sister's shoulder a brotherly squeeze. "The thing is," he told her with oily ease, "I got delayed. The joint was closed before I cashed in. Eighty dollars, sis, first thing in the morning, guaranteed. Five is all I need to tide me over," and his voice sank to nearly a whisper.

Miss Hannigan stiffened and shrugged his arm off her shoulder. "Not even a nickel for the subway."

"They got a sucker at Hennessey's tonight," pleaded Rooster, his little skinny bantam body writhing with the effort of extracting money. "I can't get in the game without a five."

"She ain't good for a lousy five bucks?" demanded Miss Hannigan, meaning Lily St. Regis. As she dropped the remark, she turned to see Lily easing another necklace down the already bulging front of her shiny dress. In the wink of an eye, Miss Hannigan was across the room and grabbing at her precious jewels. She began to pull them off Lily's wrists and fingers and drag them out of the cleavage of Lily's dress.

"I beg your pardon, I'm sure, but I don't stoop to what you're incinerating," complained Lily, unable to suppress a little whimper as she saw the baubles returning to their owner.

Furious, Miss Hannigan dumped her jewelry in a dresser drawer, and turned, grabbing up her purse.

"Rooster, if I give you five, will you take the girl out of here?"

But Rooster was already backing toward the door, grabbing Lily by the hand. "Hey. Just joking," he said quickly. "I don't need cash. I just dropped by to say howdy doody. Not even a nickel for the subway. C'mon, Lily. Say good-bye." And Rooster in his tight loud suit and Lily in her tight loud dress were gone.

Miss Hannigan was happy to see the last of them, but something wasn't quite kosher. It wasn't like Rooster Hannigan to turn down an unearned five, not even when he was holding. Unless . . . Miss Hannigan tore open her purse and looked inside. Empty. The rotten so-and-so had taken every cent while her back was turned and she was reclaiming her jewelry. That snake in the grass! That toadstool! That . . . that . . . that . . .

"Rooster!" Miss Hannigan exploded, and she threw her door open, scattering orphans like flower petals, and took off after her thieving brother. But the street was empty.

Although she had looked forward to sleeping in the huge bed, she hadn't been able to close her eyes. All her life, Annie had been accustomed to sleeping in a room with six or eight other little girls. In this vast and empty room there was no breathing besides hers and Sandy's, no whimpers or little cries in the night, no gentle snoring from childish noses. It was too quiet, too creepy, and by far too lonely. Annie's arms ached to hug Molly; she would even have been glad to see Pepper. Instead, she held tightly to Sandy, who had joined her under the covers, but even his presence and his warmth didn't comfort her enough to let her sleep. Even the Dream didn't help; in the luxury of these surroundings, Annie couldn't evoke it.

Oliver Warbucks' house, set far back from the street behind high stone walls, was isolated from its neighbors. Surrounded by extensive gardens, it was more of an estate than merely a mansion, and one had the feeling, especially at night, when the wind blew around it and the shadows of the tall trees made odd moving patterns on the bedroom ceilings, that one was far from New York City. Annie had this feeling now, sitting up in her bed, her eyes wide with fear, her little hands entwined in Sandy's fur. He wasn't feeling too comfortable himself. It seemed to Annie that Sandy was sensing something. His ears were alert, pricked at every sound, and every few minutes he whined restlessly.

"This room is bigger'n Grant's Tomb," whispered Annie into his furry ear. "Think we're ever goin' to get to sleep?"

Sandy growled in answer.

"Me either," agreed Annie, throwing back the covers and slipping her feet to the floor. Sandy barked loudly in agreement, and scrambled after her, knocking over a huge areca palm tree, scattering leaves and dirt on the carpet.

"Shhhhhh," cautioned Annie, leading the way out of the bedroom.

The hour was late, and the house was very dark and still, except for a light streaming from beneath a closed door at the end of the long corridor. It was Oliver Warbucks' office, and in it he and Grace Farrell were still working. These were the billionaire's favorite hours, when the rest of the world slept. These were the hours when, without interruption, he could get the massive amount of accumulating paperwork out of the way. He could also stay in touch with Europe and the Far East, which were either hours behind or hours ahead of the United States.

Annie

A Girl's Best Friend
Annie and Sandy

**Just an old meanie
Carol Burnett as
"Miss Hannigan"**

**Everybody's favorite orphan
Introducing Aileen Quinn as
"Annie"**

**A lovable and heroic mutt
"Sandy"**

**The Bad Guys, "Lily" and "Roost
Bernadette Peters and Tim Cur**

Everybody's favorite billionaire
Albert Finney as "'Daddy' Warbucks"

A kind new friend
for Annie
Ann Reinking as
"Grace Farrell"

"Why would anybody want to be
an orphan?"

The Magnificent
"Punjab"
Geoffrey Holder

Hail to the Chief!
FDR (and Eleanor, too)

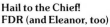

Annie comforts little Molly

"It's a hard-knock life"

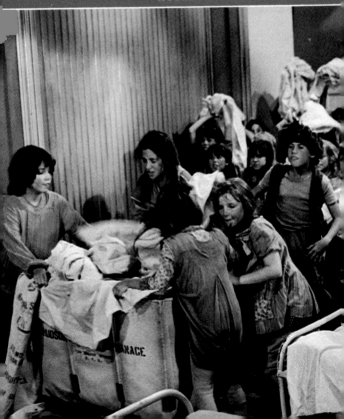

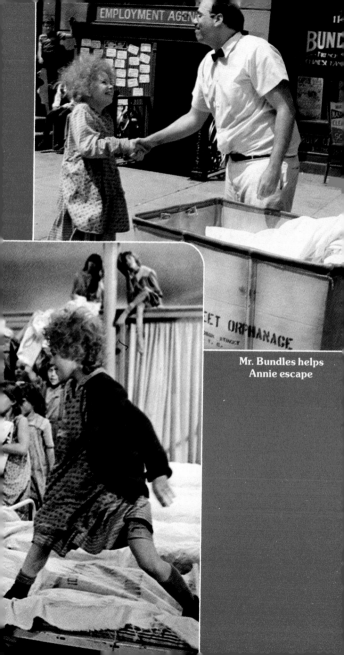

**Mr. Bundles helps
Annie escape**

And a left to the jaw!

An historic meeting—
Annie rescues Sandy

Watch those bullies run!

Answering to his name

Miss Farrell wants to "borrow" an orphan

Caught! It's back to the Home for Annie

It may not be Buckingham
Palace, but it's home
to Oliver Warbucks

u're our guest, Annie"

Annie tells Warbucks she can't be his little girl…

…and he searches for her parents

Annie's real parents? Watch out!

The orphans and Sandy bring a warning

The Bad Guys have Annie in their clutches

Leapin' Lizards!
Annie and
her rescuer

Together Forever,
Annie and her 'Daddy'

His energies flowed strongly during those hours, and Miss Farrell, being young, had learned to conquer her own weariness and keep pace with his output.

Slipping quietly down the corridor, Annie opened the door only wide enough for Sandy and her to wriggle inside. If Warbucks saw them come in, he gave no sign, but Grace raised her head and placed one admonishing finger on her lips. Annie nodded; she hadn't come for conversation, only to be near other human beings and hear the sound of voices. She didn't mind being invisible, and she kept a low profile as she and Sandy edged their way to the big leather chair in the corner, and crept into it, snuggling down together, Annie feeling safe at last, although Sandy still appeared nervous.

Oliver Warbucks was dictating at a rapid pace, and Grace Farrell's pencil was fairly flying over the pages of her steno book.

". . . In conclusion, because your country has raised its voice loud and clear for freedom and democracy," he was saying, "I will extend to you a credit line for the acquisition of thirty-five fighter planes. They come with a year's supply of spare parts, ammunition and advisers . . . What's this?"

Annie opened her eyes to find Warbucks glaring at her and Sandy, Grace looking apologetic.

"Sandy's not used to sleeping in a room all by himself," explained Annie almost truthfully.

As if to corroborate her statement, Sandy gave a low whine and a growl. The hairs on his spine and the back of his neck were quite stiff.

"Makes him nervous," said Annie, stroking him, feeling the tension in the muscles of his shoulders and neck.

At this, Sandy leaped from the chair, still growling. His eyes were fixed on the windows, the tall French windows of Warbucks' study, which opened onto a stone balcony outside. Now he broke into a series of short, loud barks.

Warbucks glared at Grace in exasperation. These interruptions were all her fault! "Where were we?"

"Ammunition and advisers, sir," read Grace Farrell from her notes.

"Are you getting a lot done?" inquired Annie in a friendly voice. Despite Warbucks' gruffness, despite his preoccupations with business and power, there was something about him she liked very much, something she couldn't put a name to, but which made her sorry to be leaving him in the morning.

Oliver Warbucks turned to the little girl with the freckled face who would insist on talking while he was dictating. At the same time, that scruffy little dog of hers broke into furious barks, all of them noisily directed at the French windows, which were, of course, closed.

"I'd get more done if some people . . ." he began, then saw the look in Annie's eyes and softened his voice and his words, ". . . if Roosevelt would leave me alone. Six phone calls since I got home."

"What's he want?" asked Annie, thrilled.

"My support for the New Deal. It's laughable," scoffed Warbucks.

"He *is* the president," Annie pointed out.

Great jumping Jehoshaphat! Was the child a Democrat on top of everything else? How could Miss Farrell have . . . ?

Now Sandy's barking was incessant and frantic, and Warbucks gave up. "Punjab!" he roared, wanting the dog taken away at once.

What happened next was too fast and too furious and too confusing to sort out right away. At his command, Punjab and the Asp rushed into the room, but instead of grabbing at Sandy, they flew past him, toward the French windows. There was a smashing sound and the tinkle of glass as a round black bomb, its fuse lit, flew through the window, hit the floor and began to roll toward Warbucks. The Asp made a dive for the bomb, snatched it up and threw it in a lateral pass to Punjab, who nearly fumbled it but recovered and dashed with it out of the room. The Asp threw open the French windows to catch a departing glimpse of the wild-eyed bearded anarchist disappearing over the balcony. At once, Sandy leaped through the windows and after the radical.

Through all of this commotion, Oliver Warbucks didn't miss a beat. Although Annie and Grace ran to the door after Punjab, Warbucks didn't stir. With a sigh of exasperation at all the commotion, he picked up the microphone to his dictating machine and switched it on.

"A letter on my personal stationery to Miss Emmeline Bush, Smith College, Northampton, Mass. Dear Emmy . . ."

Outside the door, an unmuffled boom as the bomb exploded harmlessly. Punjab came back, dusting his hands, followed by Annie and Grace. Outside, on the balcony, Sandy and the Asp had their paws and hands full. Sandy had dragged the Red Menace back up the balcony by the cuffs of his pants, but the man was armed to the teeth and putting up quite a fight. Sandy kept his teeth buried in the man's leg, but the Asp couldn't get close enough for a karate chop. However, as soon as Punjab joined them on the balcony, the fight was over, and the glowering, cursing anarchist was marched into the office, subdued.

"It has come to my attention," continued Warbucks into the Dictaphone, "that you have spent the five thousand dollars I gave you to purchase a horse for Madison Square Garden. Emmy, dear, that money was for schoolbooks and next year's tuition. Only my affection for your mother prevents me from being very angry. It is not enough in this uncertain age for a young woman to know nothing but how to set a table and sit a horse. I am willing to subsidize your studies in anthropology, but only if you're willing to study anthropology. Your mother and I lunch regularly every other Saturday at the Plaza. Meet us there. We need to sort this out. Your exasperated Uncle Oliver."

Annie watched wide-eyed as Punjab and the Asp marched Warbucks' would-be assassin through the office, and out to the police. She glanced at Grace, whose face was pale and who was breathing hard, now that the excitement was over. Grace was staring at Warbucks with mingled fear and relief showing strongly on her usually placid features. It suddenly became apparent to Annie that Miss Farrell's constant solicitude for her employer might have little to do with the salary she was paid. Annie looked at Warbucks, but he was still busy with his dictating.

"P.S. I assume you are riding some embarrassing saddle held together with baling wire and safety pins. This is not acceptable equipment for Madison Square Garden. This too must be discussed."

He hung the microphone back on its rack and turned his attention to the pile of letters that needed his signature. Annie, who was just beginning to recover from the ninety seconds of peak excitement, moved slowly to the desk. She was still puzzled.

"What was that all about?"

Warbucks glanced up casually, as though nothing had happened, but one hand dropped below and patted Sandy on the head.

"Not bad, Taffy," he acknowledged, which from Warbucks was the highest possible praise.

"Sandy," corrected Annie automatically. "Was that man trying to kill you?"

Grace came and took Annie by the hand, leading her gently out of the room.

"Who'd want to kill Mr. Warbucks?" asked Annie again. She was completely bewildered; everything had happened so fast, and without a word being spoken in explanation.

"The Bolsheviks," Grace told her. "Mr. Warbucks is the living proof that the American system works."

"The Bolsheviks," whispered Annie, shuddering. The little she had gleaned about them from Miss Hannigan's radio had led the orphans to imagine them with gleaming fangs, horns, and tails. Not to mention bombs. Well, she'd seen the bomb, all right, and she was willing to bet there was a tail under those ragged black clothes. "Leapin' lizards!" she whistled. Then, turning back to him, she asked the billionaire, "You want Sandy to sleep with you, Mr. Warbucks?"

Warbucks' eyes popped open in dismay. "Good Lord, no!" he gasped, showing more anxiety than he had when the bomb came through the window. "I never sleep with a dog if I can avoid it."

Annie nodded and went off to bed, where she curled up with the heroic Sandy and went promptly to sleep, tuckered out from the excitement.

In his office, Oliver Warbucks turned to Grace Farrell and asked quietly, "Shall we resume?"

"Of course, sir," and she took her place at the other side of the desk, her pencil poised over her note pad. She was her usual calm, efficient self again, but there was something unspoken between them. Both of them knew that Annie would not be going back to the Hudson Street Home in the morning, or be traded in for some boy orphan. She'd be finishing out her week.

When Oliver Warbucks did anything, he never did it by halves. The next morning Annie was awakened by a small parade into her bedroom, led by Miss Farrell, and made up of Cecille and Annette carrying large boxes from Best and Company and De Pinna. In them were more clothes than Annie had seen in all of her ten years. Dresses for daytime, crisp with pleats and sailor collars, with smocking and puffed sleeves. Dresses for dinnertime, of rich blue or maroon velvet with lace-edged collars and tiny pearl buttons. And Annie's special favorite, a plain tailored red dress with a set-in belt and a white piqué pilgrim collar. It was the exact color of her old red sweater, and Annie knew she'd be wearing it a lot. There were outfits for riding, snappy little jodhpurs and a velvet-collared jacket of hunting pink. There were tennis dresses for her lessons with Don Budge, short white skirts and sweaters with little white socks to match. There was even a golfing costume, with tiny plus fours, an argyle sweater and a fuzzy cap. There was dainty underwear of cotton batiste, nightgowns with rosebuds embroidered on them, and, for later in the year, a darling little brown tweed coat trimmed in brown velvet, with velvet-trimmed leggings to match, and a little velvet bonnet and muff so dear that Annie gave a squeak of joy when they were unpacked. And there was more, much more.

Annie thought she'd never come to the bottoms of the boxes, so jammed with wonderful things were they. Grace Farrell sat on the edge of Annie's bed as the child went through the mounds of tissue paper. She was enjoying Annie's pleasure almost as much as the little girl was enjoying her new possessions.

"Gee, Miss Farrell, I never seen so many beautiful things in my life!" Then the tiny face clouded. "I hope Miss Hannigan will let me keep some of them. At least the red dress."

Miss Hannigan's name threw a momentary chill over both their hearts. Even though both of them knew this visit was to be short, they'd pushed that knowledge as far away as they could.

"Oh, I'm certain she will, dear," said Miss Farrell comfortingly. *She will if I have anything to say about it,* she thought to herself grimly. Yet, she knew how absurd these luxurious outfits would be in an orphanage, how impractical. She hoped with all her heart that they weren't doing Annie any harm by taking her out of her old life for a week. But just to see the child so happy! Although they'd known each other for only a day, Miss Farrell felt a deep fondness for Annie beginning to grow.

As for Annie, she had never met anybody as sweet or as warm as Grace Farrell. It wouldn't be only the luxury she'd miss, going back to the Hudson Street Home for Girls, it would be the kindly presence of Miss Farrell. And, yes, she'd miss Oliver Warbucks, too. He wasn't quite as scary as she'd been led to picture. Not at all. She remembered the gentle pat and the quiet word of praise he'd given Sandy last night, and she knew there was more of the same buried in him somewhere, just waiting to come out.

Sandy, of course, would miss the luxury. He'd been shampooed and de-flead and was basking in his new cleanliness, a warm breakfast making a comforting lump in his stomach. Who said it was a dog's life?

Breakfast was the first thing on Annie's agenda for today, but when she'd been led down the stairs to the imposing dining room that seated forty, with its sixty-foot-long table set for one, her heart quailed. Mr. Warbucks and Miss Farrell had had their breakfast hours ago, and Annie faced a solitary meal, if you didn't count the footmen waiting on her. She slipped away from the table and ran down the service steps to the huge, warm, bright kitchen, and begged Mrs. Pugh to let her eat there, at the scrubbed pine kitchen table. The kitchen was bustling with activity and good smells—fresh bread baking for lunch, onions being fried. How could Mrs. Pugh refuse her?

So Annie ate her bacon and eggs and whole-wheat toast with orange marmalade and drank her fresh-squeezed grapefruit juice and a tall glass of milk with the best appetite she'd ever had. And even Sandy, after a hairy moment or two with Mrs. Pugh's cat, who wasn't about to share her kitchen with this loutish beast, settled under

Annie's chair, contentedly gnawing a bone. This would set the pattern for her future breakfasts. Lunch she'd take with Miss Farrell, and dinner was served early in her room, but breakfasts were eaten in the kitchen, just as they should always be.

After she finished her meal and had mopped the last bit of egg yolk off her plate with the last bite of toast, Annie wandered through the ground floor of the mansion, marveling at everything she looked at. Of course, she wasn't educated to appreciate art, her eye had never been trained nor her taste formed by experts, but Annie was quick to learn, quick to appreciate, and had a warm feeling for beauty. She stopped to gaze at landscapes by Turner, portraits by Gainsborough, religious paintings by El Greco and Memling, without knowing the first thing about them. Yet she recognized them as unique and special. But the picture that caught her eye and her heart was a soft study of a lovely woman and her little daughter, dressed in matching bonnets and the styles of forty years ago. Their faces were plump and very pretty, and their lips were very red, their eyes a velvet black; they looked alike. The painter, a man named Auguste Renoir, had captured the affection between the two in the casual depiction of the child's arm around her mother's neck, and the mother's caressing glance at her little girl. The picture brought a surprising lump to Annie's throat, she wanted to reach into it and touch them both, even to join them for a few minutes and learn their names. What she wanted most was to have a share in that affection, to feel a mother's arms. She tore herself away from the painting with a promise to come back to it tomorrow.

The library of Oliver Warbucks was like nothing she had ever imagined. It seemed to be two stories high, and books were shelved so close to the ceiling that a little ladder on wheels had to be used to fetch them from the topmost shelves. There must have been twelve or thirteen thousand books in that room with its painted pilasters and marble facings, and all of them were bound in green leather, their titles and authors and the initials O.W. stamped on their spines in gold. Annie was afraid to touch one, much as she longed to.

A long table in the library was covered with newspapers

in twenty-three foreign languages, and picture magazines from all over the world. Annie leafed through these, and the events of the day leaped out at her in pictures. A lot of the photographs had to do with Germany, where a new chancellor had been elected, a man named Adolf Hitler, who dressed his followers in paramilitary style, with brown shirts and armbands. The pictures of Hitler gave Annie a creepy feeling; she couldn't tell why. But she sure didn't like his face.

She put the magazines back on the table and turned her attention to a globe nearly as big as she was, a map of the world that was entirely up to date, with little colored pins stuck in it all over, representing Oliver Warbucks' farflung business empire. His interests spanned the huge globe—oil, rubber, manganese, diamonds, uranium ore, gold, silver, copper, tin, coal, iron, sugar, cocoa, tea, coffee, saffron, silk—there was nothing grown, dug, mined, drilled anywhere in the world that Oliver Warbucks didn't have a share in. The black pins represented his factories, and Annie saw to her astonishment that he had mills and manufactories as far away as Alaska, Hong Kong, Fiji, Rumania, Scotland, and India. Wow! There was so much to see and do, so much to learn, how was she ever going to cram it in, with only a week?

A footman appeared silently in the doorway, asking if Annie would care to join Mr. Warbucks in the swimming pool. Would she! She was up in her room in ten seconds, had changed into her bathing suit in thirty more, and was at poolside fastening on her rubber bathing cap before two minutes had gone by.

Oliver Warbucks was swimming underwater when Annie arrived. Sandy took one horrified look and dived in head-first without hesitation, swimming toward Warbucks and seizing the billionaire's backside in his teeth, hauling him up to the surface in another daring rescue.

"Get your dog out of my pool!" shouted the billionaire indignantly. The humiliation of being dragged to the surface by a dog!

"He thought you were drowning," called Annie. "Like my suit?" She was very proud of her first bathing suit; it was a bright yellow that set off the color of her hair and her pale skin.

"What? Oh, yes."

"Miss Farrell picked it out," said Annie, sticking one toe into the water.

"That's nice," said Warbucks without much interest. He was concentrating on his backstroke, which needed a little work.

Annie slid into the water and paddled toward the billionaire. "She's got a really good eye, don'tcha think? She really knows what looks good on a person, don'tcha think?" She watched for Warbucks' reaction to her praise of Miss Farrell, but not much was forthcoming. "I mean this looks just about perfect on me, don'tcha think?" It was evident that this line of conversation wasn't getting them anywhere.

But, while Warbucks wasn't actually listening to what Annie was saying, he *was* in fact paying attention to her. To her liveliness, her quick smile, her lack of fear, her obvious intelligence. He swam over next to her, and gave her rubber-capped head an awkward pat, much the same kind as the one he'd given Sandy.

"I never thought I'd get used to a girl," he said in mild astonishment.

"Girls are easier to get used to than boys," replied Annie with some complacence. She was reveling in the pat. "Look how used to Miss Farrell you are. She does all the work around here and you don't even know her first name."

Warbucks uttered a short, barking laugh. "I do. It's Grace," he said, as he swam toward the pool steps. He climbed up and shook the excess water off him, while Annie floated on her back and admired him. He was a man in splendid physical condition, with a barrel chest and a strong pair of legs. He wore an old-fashioned two-piece tank suit of black wool, mixed with something new he was developing, a synthetic called "nylon," which he was certain would revolutionize fabric technology. Nylon dried quickly, due to its molecular construction, and someday every bathing suit in the world would be entirely or partially made of it. Now he reached for his long terry-cloth robe.

"She thinks you're the greatest thing since sliced bread," called Annie.

Warbucks' head jerked around to stare at the child in astonishment. What the devil was she talking about? Miss Farrell? Sliced bread? "I beg your pardon?" he asked, somewhat stiffly.

"I know it's none of my business," Annie went on cheerfully, "but you never notice anything." If she only had a week here, she was going to have to work fast and never mind the consequences.

Warbucks was dazed; he could barely comprehend the significance of what Annie was saying. But he had work to do; there was no time to stand around discussing sliced bread with a ten-year-old. It was with no little relief that he tied the belt of his robe and hurried out of there.

Annie's visit progressed. It even fell into something of a routine. Tennis lessons, a riding lesson, regular meals. Toys and games and books arrived from the stores in profusion, and Annie enjoyed them all. She was enjoying everything, what orphan wouldn't? Sandy was putting on weight and was losing some of that hangdog look. Even his bark was more authoritative.

Annie was making friends. The maids and the footmen loved her. Mrs. Pugh adored her, especially the way she cleaned her plate and asked for more. She took to preparing special goodies for Annie. Poor Annie! She would have preferred a steak or a turkey leg any day, but Mrs. Pugh took to stuffing her with Lobster Thermidor, Frog's Legs Provençale, Sweetbreads in Madeira. But Annie drew the line at Calves' Brains with Caper Sauce, and Mrs. Pugh fried her a hamburger instead.

Even Drake, who relied upon his dignity as head butler to see him through life's crises—and there is no dignity in the world, not a king's or even a pope's, as complete and unassailable as the dignity of a head butler—unbent a little now in Annie's presence, and was once seen to—almost—smile. Sandy, of course, was still beyond the pale as far as Drake was concerned, but at least he didn't make Drake sneeze anymore, now that he was bathed daily.

Although one could never tell what the Asp was thinking, Annie felt that he liked her. In between his duties as chauffeur and bodyguard to Oliver Warbucks, he managed to sandwich sessions with Annie, during which he taught her, swiftly and silently, certain centuries-old secrets of self-defense. How to deliver a deadly blow with the back of one's hand; where the vital points on an enemy's body were; how to come and go so silently as to almost become invisible—all very useful information for a ten-year-old girl.

With Punjab, however, Annie had a very special relationship. They adored each other. He called her Princess. From the very first minute, when he'd taken her hand in his and looked deeply into her eyes, they'd had a very special friendship, this nine-foot-tall Indian and the four-foot-high orphan. It was as though they had been linked together in an earlier life, and knew each other very well. Punjab seemed to know everything in the world—ahead of time—and sometimes, with a magical pass of his huge hands, he did Indian fakir tricks for Annie's delight. The immense power of his huge body turned to gentleness whenever he was with Annie. Sandy, who was still the tiniest bit wary of the Asp, was melted butter where Punjab was concerned.

Annie's affection for Grace, and Grace's for Annie, grew day by day. But that was hardly surprising, since there was a deep maternal streak in Miss Farrell, and a deep need for mothering in Annie. Besides, loving Miss Farrell was no great trick. Who couldn't love a young woman as beautiful and kind as she was? But caring for Oliver Warbucks was an entirely different matter—now *there* was a challenge. Powerful, arrogant, busy all the time, Warbucks scarcely exchanged a word with Annie. The world made heavy demands on his time and energies. Yet, despite all of this, Annie felt closer to Warbucks with every passing day. His second-floor office was the nerve center of the house; sometimes Annie thought it was the nerve center of the entire world. It was Warbucks' command post, and he ran it like a five-star general.

In addition to the latest in office equipment, Warbucks' office boasted a Wall Street ticker-tape machine, and two teletype machines, one connected to the Associated Press and the other for overseas dispatches. News from around the world arrived at once in that office, and Warbucks absorbed it all. It wasn't looking too good for the world these days, and he sometimes wondered how long he'd have to shoulder the burden of failing national economies.

There was a short-wave radio that received marine band signals as well as all the major cities of Europe, and on the wall behind Warbucks' massive walnut desk was a finely detailed map of the world with more of his pins stuck in it. Warbucks worked long, long hours in this room, making decisions that affected history.

Annie loved being with him, in his office, watching him work, and he'd grown accustomed, even in so short a time, to being with her. Something about this orphan child struck a note in the area under his watch chain in the region of the heart. Her independence and fearlessness reminded him of himself, and he had finally gotten over wishing she were a boy. Although Warbucks was used to being regarded with respect and even awe, he valued Annie's respect. Perhaps it was because he sensed that Annie, although too young to grasp the full extent of Warbucks' wealth and influence, cared little for money or power. It was Warbucks' personal power, his charisma if you like, that earned her appreciation. She liked him because he was himself, not because he was the tycoon Warbucks. For him, it was a refreshing change. He sometimes longed to be a little more relaxed, but he wasn't sure exactly how to go about it.

Warbucks was aware that time was passing very quickly, and that Annie's visit would soon be over. Sometimes he saw that fact reflected in Grace Farrell's eyes when she looked at the little girl, and he thought it was too bad, but there it was. A promise was a promise, a week was a week, and that was all there was to it. It had been a more pleasant and less taxing week than he'd imagined, but all things must come to an end, and Oliver Warbucks was a very busy man.

And, thank heaven, there had been no repetition of that uncomfortable conversation about sliced bread.

CHAPTER SIX

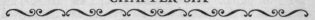

And then it was Annie's last day but one. The time had flown by so quickly, and Annie had soaked up so many wonderful memories that she thought she'd have a lifetime to take them all out over and over again to relive them. A born optimist, Annie had accepted most of the burdens of her wretched life with cheerful equanimity, certain that tomorrow would bring something better. Now tomorrow had come and was almost gone, and Annie found it hard to be cheerful. She'd always known it had to end, but now that the end was in sight, the thought of Miss Hannigan and the mean and drab discomforts of the Hudson Street Home for Girls weighed on her heavily. Certainly, she didn't expect life to be all luxury, as it was here at Warbucks', but here she had received attention, respect, and even love, and it was hard to be going back to kicks and cuffs and the scrubbing brushes and the sewing machines, with only baby Molly to love her. And Sandy, what about Sandy? Annie knew they were committed to each other, never to be parted again. But how was she going to sneak him past Miss Hannigan, who had a contract out on Sandy with the sausage factory?

Do you suppose Miss Farrell would adopt Sandy and give him a home? He'd be real good, and he could live downstairs in the kitchen. No, Mrs. Pugh's cat would never allow that. But, after all, he did help save Mr. Warbucks' life, didn't he? But if Miss Farrell gave Sandy a home, that probably meant that Annie would never see him again.

Or Miss Farrell either. Or Mr. Warbucks. Or the Asp, or dear Punjab. Best not to think of that, 'cause it made Annie feel like crying, and Annie never cried.

But on her last day but one, Annie got up extra early,

even before Annette could come in to wake her. She didn't want to waste one precious minute of the little time she had left. She raced through an early-morning swim, managed to hit three back over the net to Don Budge, rode her pony for an hour in the grounds around the mansion, ate breakfast in the kitchen with Mrs. Pugh, and still arrived at Warbucks' office on the dot of ten.

But today it seemed as though neither Miss Farrell nor Mr. Warbucks had any time for a ten-year-old orphan, even one whose tennis game was improving. The World Situation was worsening, and Warbucks was needed every minute. Frantic telephone calls kept coming in from the major cities of the world, as national leaders were turning to Oliver Warbucks for help. The ticker tape was chattering like an excited chimpanzee. Saying "Sell, sell, sell." Warbucks was on the phone ordering his brokers to buy, buy, buy. The teletype machines were going crazy, spitting out long ribbons of paper on which the news from everywhere appeared as soon as it happened.

So Annie found himself ignored. At first, she kept out of the way, sitting in the big green leather chair in the corner, her large blue eyes watching Mr. Warbucks solve the world's problems by telephone. But after a while even that became boring. Still, she was reluctant to go; she loved it here in the busy, important atmosphere of commerce, industry, and politics. If only she had something to do! Sandy, having eaten too much breakfast, was curled up asleep at her feet, while his digestion carried on without him.

Mr. Warbucks was on two telephones at the same time, and the third phone was ringing off the hook. A brace of typists, hired by the hour, was sitting at a pair of typewriters turning out memos, notes, and letters. Grace Farrell had the Dictaphone headset on and was typing Mr. Warbucks' most secret correspondence. Punjab was on guard at the door. The Asp was off heaven knows where doing heaven knows what in his silent manner. Only Annie had nothing to do.

Suddenly, her eye fell on a small desktop model of Oliver Warbucks' latest enthusiasm, his "autocopter," a plump airship with short wings and a huge gyroscopic rotor on its roof. Warbucks and a man named Igor Ivan

Sikorsky were experimenting with it, and Warbucks intended to put it into production within three months; a factory hidden in Wyoming was tooling up for it even now, and nobody in Europe had seen anything like it. It was a craft that didn't need an airfield or even a landing strip; it lifted straight up, hovered, went backwards or forwards, and could land on a dime by coming straight down. The prototype was sitting even now on Warbucks' roof, and the model was sitting on his desk.

Quick as lightning, Annie had the model in her hand and was playing "aeroplane" with it, silently at first, making *"RRRRRRRRRR"* engine noises under her breath. But she was soon caught up in her game, and flying the 'copter noisily around Warbucks' office, around everybody's head. Punjab watched her with delight for a few minutes, then, he, too, joined in the game. Without leaving his post, he waved one hand in the air, and a World War I fighter plane model took off from its stand and began circling the room, its miniature guns blazing. With a whoop of joy, Annie chased it, the autocopter in her hand. Bedlam broke out. The phones kept ringing, the secretaries typing, the dog snoring, the tiny planes barking bullets at each other.

"Ambassador," Warbucks was shouting into one of the phones, "I'm not prepared to bicker over price! That young lunatic, Hitler, is a real threat, whether you see it or not. I make the best fighter in the air. I would advise you either to pay my price or to learn German!"

He slammed down the phone, and the little fighter plane model zoomed low, narrowly missing Warbucks' bald skull. He scowled in annoyance.

"Don't encourage her, Punjab."

Punjab bowed his head obediently and waved two fingers in the air. At once, the little plane flew to its perch and settled there, its guns silent.

Warbucks snatched up the second phone. "Hello? Who is this?" he demanded. "Oh, Wilhelm. Let me call you back."

Annie was now firing on an aircraft carrier model, making the kind of racket only a ten-year-old in a war game can make. Warbucks rested his elbows on the desk and clasped his head in both hands.

Grace leaped to her feet. "Maybe I could take her out, Mr. Warbucks."

"Good idea," nodded Warbucks vigorously. "Annie, where do you want to go?"

Annie turned a shining, excited face to him.

"To Washington," she said with certainty. "To meet President Roosevelt."

Too late, Annie saw that Warbucks' eyes were cold as gray iron and that his jaw was an angry knot framed by a scowl. Roosevelt! That Man in the White House! Warbucks despised him, considering him a traitor to his class and a know-nothing do-gooder. Annie laughed nervously. "Sorry, sir."

"How about a movie?" asked Grace quickly.

Annie gasped in excitement. She'd never seen a movie, but she'd heard about the miracle of talking pictures. "Pepper went to a movie once, before she came to the orphanage. She said it was swell. And Miss Hannigan goes all the time."

"Splendid!" Warbucks nodded decisively. "Take her to Radio City Music Hall."

Annie's eyes stung and her lower lip trembled a little.

"I thought *you* were gonna take me," she said to Mr. Warbucks.

Warbucks uttered an indulgent laugh. "Me? Annie, you may think Miss Farrell does all the work around here, but it's not entirely true. I'm a busy man. A very busy man."

Annie's face fell. "I know," she said quietly. "I didn't mean to get in the way, Mr. Warbucks. Nobody has to take me anywhere. I'll go practice my backhand." She turned and headed slowly for the door, Grace biting her lip as she watched Annie go. But she didn't dare say anything.

At the door, Annie stopped and threw them a tiny smile.

"Pepper lies a lot. She probably hasn't been to a movie ever either." Her smiled widened a little as she looked clearly at Mr. Warbucks.

"Actually, I think it's better when you don't know what you're missing," she declared.

Warbucks felt something move inside him. Not pity; Annie never wanted pity. Not even sympathy. It was more like . . . empathy . . . it moved, was gone, leaving him feeling a little empty.

"Punjab!" he shouted suddenly. "Buy out the eight P.M. show. Let's *all* go to the movies!" He felt suddenly rewarded by the grin that appeared like magic on Annie's freckled face, and, oddly enough, by the smile on Grace Farrell's.

Dinner was early that night so they could make the show. Annie could hardly eat for excitement, and she was so overwhelmed by it all that she was almost silent at the table. But her dancing eyes did the talking for her, and Warbucks, watching her, felt younger than he had in years. He couldn't remember the last film he'd seen, probably a Charlie Chaplin silent movie. The talkies were only three years old; he discovered he was eager to see one.

After dinner, Annie went to Grace Farrell's room to watch her get dressed. In her pink silk slip, she looked very different from the prim young woman in the business suit. For one thing, her waist was thinner and her bosom fuller than appeared in her tailored clothing. And, for another, her hair was down.

Annie had never seen such beautiful hair, silky and thick and a soft golden brown with reddish highlights. She yearned to touch it, and begged Miss Farrell to let her brush it for her. Back at the orphanage, she brushed and combed Molly's hair all the time and because this was Annie's last evening, Grace permitted it. She sat down at her dressing table with Annie standing behind her. For a few minutes, nothing was said. The girl brushed the lovely hair with gentle but sure strokes, and the young woman watched her in the mirror, thoughts sadly on the next morning.

At last, Annie had finished, and Grace took up the pretty handfuls and began to roll them up in her usual neat coiffure.

"Ah, leave your hair down," begged Annie. "It's so pretty."

"Annie, I couldn't," protested Grace with an embarrassed laugh, and stuck the pins quickly into her hair, securing it modestly.

"Miss Hannigan says a man don't look at your brains,"

remarked Annie, provoking a blush from Miss Farrell. Together they went through Grace's clothes closet, looking for something to wear. Grace pulled out hanger after hanger, but Annie kept shaking her head in disapproval. Everything Miss Farrell had was either dark gray, dark blue, dark brown, or tweed, and everything was man-tailored! At last, Grace found a light silk dress, demure in cut, but of a lovely soft material, in gunmetal gray. Putting her head to one side, Annie regarded it judiciously for a minute, then gave a reluctant nod of approval. She would much rather have had red.

But once the dress was on, Annie uttered a little admiring whistle. The demurely cut little nothing of a dress clung to Miss Farrell's slender shape in all the right places, and the slivery gray color set off the gray of her eyes and the roses that had suddenly appeared in her cheeks. Annie made Miss Farrell take a good long look at herself in the mirror, and both of them liked what they saw.

They stood side by side, looking at their reflections in the glass. There was not the slightest resemblance between them, and yet they looked somehow right together. As if they belonged together, the skinny little redheaded girl and the silvery gray color set off the gray of her eyes and Grace gave Annie's hand an extra squeeze as they left her room and went down to join Oliver Warbucks in the library.

Warbucks was sipping a rare Napoleon brandy and contemplating the pins in the globe as they came in the door, and his startled glance at Miss Farrell gave Annie a stab of pleasure. He was noticing her at last, as a person, not as an efficient piece of office equipment. He was noticing for the first time that Grace Farrell was one very pretty lady, and Annie felt partly responsible. She was very proud; her week here might have some good effects after all.

But now it was magic time, time to go to the movies. The Dusenberg was waiting at the front door with the Asp at the wheel. Punjab was ready to escort them, and even Sandy was wearing a brand-new leather collar. In her red dress and black Mary-Jane shoes, Annie felt quite the lady as Punjab stepped back to let her pass. They all climbed into the car and the Asp stepped on the gas.

It was a beautiful evening, the Dusenberg's convertible

top was down, and before they knew it they were pulling up to the brand-new Radio City Music Hall, showcase of the stars and home of the famous stage show featuring the Rockettes. Or so it said on the marquee, and Annie for one was ready to believe it. Huge signs posted in the lobby informed the public that the eight o'clock show was completely sold out. It was now three minutes to eight. The ticket man accepted their tickets with a bow.

When they stepped into the lobby, Annie's heart did a little jump of sheer surprise. Even the incredible luxury of Oliver Warbucks' mansion hadn't prepared her for the vast sweep of the Radio City Music Hall lobby. It was four stories high, and totally carpeted in what felt like velvet underfoot. Across the vast expanse of carpet, a staircase wound up to the higher floors, but of course there were elevators to take people as high as they wanted to go, or at least as high as their tickets entitled them to go. It was all decorated in the latest style, art moderne, as it was called then. The pictures on the walls, the huge murals, the magnificence of the chandelier and the other lighting fixtures, the sweep of the balustrade, all these made Annie gasp in wonder. Even Warbucks was impressed; they didn't call this a picture palace for nothing.

A little overawed, Annie slipped her hand into Mr. Warbucks', and he took it in his, marveling to himself how small and fragile it seemed to be.

An army of ushers and attendants was there to greet them, wearing magnificent uniforms trimmed in gold braid, with large gold shoulderboards and shiny gold buttons. As they were handed their programs, Punjab stepped up to the candy counter and filled his hands with Raisinets, Good and Plenty, two boxes of Dots, and Bonomo's Turkish Taffy, all guaranteed to last through the picture and the stage show.

The head usher, in the uniform of a full colonel in the Bulgarian cavalry, showed them to their seats in the beam of his flashlight. They were close to the stage.

Annie looked around. Apart from their party, the vast movie theater was entirely empty.

"Where is everybody else?" she whispered to Grace Farrell.

"Mr. Warbucks bought out the house," Grace whispered back.

Suddenly, an eerie light began to play and a swell of music came from nowhere. Sandy uttered a hoarse bark of terror, and Annie crouched low in her seat.

The music was coming from the left-hand corner of the stage, and in a moment they saw, to their wonderment, an organ rise majestically out of the pit, with a man at the keyboard. He was playing "Lady of Spain," pulling out all the stops in great quavers and vox humana. After another selection and an encore, an orchestra broke into the *William Tell Overture* as it, too, rose out of the pit, bathed in colored lights. Annie had never even imagined anything like it.

The stage show was heaven, with dancers, clowns, jugglers, Chinese acrobats, a lady on a trampoline, and even a roller-skating bear. There was a dog act in which poodles wearing ruffled clothing walked around on their hind legs balancing things, while Sandy, not too appreciative, growled low in his throat, and Annie wondered if she could get Sandy to jump through a paper hoop with a little American flag in his teeth.

And the Rockettes—what words could Annie use to tell about them back at the orphanage? And how would they ever believe her? Here was an incredible line of fifty of the world's most beautiful women, dressed in daring costumes covered in spangles and sequins, and dancing with the precision of an army drill team, kicking up their legs in perfect unison, and making it appear so very easy! Annie wriggled with joy in her seat, and never wanted them to stop dancing.

But at last the show was over, and it was time for the movie itself to begin. But before that, a cartoon, Annie's very first cartoon, a Mickey Mouse called *Steamboat Willie*. What bliss! And then a newsreel, and a trailer for the next big feature and, at last, the movie! By now, Annie was so exhausted by the entire thrilling experience that her eyes were beginning to shut.

The film was a love story, in which Greta Garbo, surely the most beautiful woman in the world, suffered for love. Her boyfriend, Robert Taylor, surely the most beautiful man in the world, also suffered for love, but in his case it was harder to tell, because his facial expressions didn't change all that much. Annie found the film a little difficult to follow, because there was so much mushy love stuff in it, and after fifteen minutes of "Armand, Armand," and "Marguerite, my adored one," she fell fast asleep in her seat. In the seat next to hers, Sandy had given up during the disasters in the newsreel and was snoring gently.

Had Annie stayed awake, she would have seen something a lot more interesting than what was going on up there on the silver screen. As Marguerite died in the arms of her lover, Grace Farrell, who had been weeping silently during most of the movie, broke out into loud, gasping sobs, and Oliver Warbucks was patting her shoulder and handing her his handkerchief. Not only that, he was looking rather pleased with himself.

When the movie was over, Punjab lifted the sleeping Annie and, cradling her gently in his arms so as not to waken her, carried her out to the car and placed her on the back seat. She slept on, and so did Sandy.

But when they arrived home, Mr. Warbucks would not let Punjab carry her into the house and up the stairs. Instead, he lifted her himself, marveling at how light she was, and, with Grace following, carried her upstairs and into her room.

He helped Grace take off Annie's shoes and socks and, under Grace's expert guidance, managed to get Annie out of her clothes and into her nightdress without waking the child. He noticed as he did so that Annie was still wearing that broken little locket on a chain he'd seen when first he laid eyes on her. Indeed, she'd never had it off. One would think that with all the beautiful new possessions she'd acquired, she'd throw away the useless thing.

"You certainly are efficient," he praised Miss Farrell, who was looking . . . different . . . tonight. "I don't know how you manage to do everything. I don't know anything at all about children; I could never put one to bed."

Grace threw him a ravishing smile.

"Why, Mr. Warbucks, what an odd thing to say. You just did!"

He looked down at Annie. She was still sound asleep, her red curls tumbled on the pillow. The sight of her peaceful little face touched him mightily. He was glad he hadn't swapped her for a boy.

"Why, yes," he said slowly. "I did, didn't I? I put her to bed."

Smiling at each other, they left the room and shut the door quietly behind them. Annie slept on.

CHAPTER SEVEN

Her last day. Today is the day Annie goes back to the
Hudson Street Home for Girls, Established 1891. Today is
the day she goes back to being cold in the winter, hot in
the summer, hungry all year round, unloved and lonely.
Today is the day she says good-bye to everything and
everybody she has come to care about and is delivered
back into the clutches of Miss Hannigan, who hates her.
Miss Hannigan has been waiting for one solid week to
work out her hostilities and frustrations on the bodies of
one small redheaded child and a dog.

Is it any wonder that Annie is sleeping late?

She had planned to get up as early as the day before, to
enjoy every last minute of her last day. But when day
broke, Annie couldn't face it, and burrowed deeply into
her pillow.

And it was a beautiful day, too, with balmy tempera-
tures, soft breezes, sunshine. Oliver Warbucks decided to
have his breakfast in the garden, which was something of a
departure for him, because he usually didn't notice the
weather or his surroundings. But he was still Warbucks, so
he ordered the ticker-tape machine brought to his table,
and, while the birds sang in the trees and the squirrels
packed their cheeks with seeds and berries, Warbucks
sipped his scalding black coffee and studied the stock
market quotations intently. He might have been in a bro-
kerage office for all he noticed the garden now that he was
in it, for the stock market figures were looking particularly
black today.

Carrying the silver coffeepot filled with fresh brew,
Grace Farrell came into the garden. She matched the flowers with her beauty this morning, for she had left her hair
flowing to her shoulders, and had pinned a blooming tea

rose on the lapel of her jacket, close to her cheek, where its perfume might reach her nose.

"She's still asleep," she told the scowling Warbucks. "That was a wonderful evening you gave her." She waited for a reply, a nod, a smile, but none of those were forthcoming. Instead, Warbucks muttered something dire at the ticker tape.

This was going to make things a lot more difficult for what Grace intended. But she had made her mind up to speak, after spending a restless night wrestling with the new idea. She took a deep breath.

"Sir, I was wondering—" she began, but Warbucks cut her off without listening.

"I'm going to have to close the factory in Pittsburgh, Grace," he said. It was the first time he'd ever called her by her first name, and she felt a brief thrill of pleasure.

"About Annie—" she began again.

"What about Annie?" asked Warbucks brusquely. He, too, knew what day this was.

"Could we keep her?" She hadn't meant to blurt it out like that, but to lead up to it tactfully. Still, there it was, spoken between them. She looked eagerly into the billionaire's face for some encouragement.

But there was no encouragement there. Warbucks' scowl cut deeper into his face, and he gave an impatient shake of his head.

But Grace wasn't frightened off . . . yet. This was too important to her.

"You haven't seen that horrible orphanage," she pleaded. "I can't bear to send her back there."

"What's come over you, Grace? Get hold of yourself," snapped Warbucks, looking acutely uncomfortable.

"You have plenty of room," she persisted. "The staff adores her. She wouldn't be a bother, I'll look after her. She could live here as . . . well . . . as your ward. Couldn't she?"

Warbucks shook his head irritably. "Absolutely not. I'm a businessman. I love money. I love power. I love capitalism. I do not now and never will love children." It certainly sounded final.

Fighting back tears, Grace stood up. She turned to go, hesitated, then turned back, for a final feeble try.

"Watching you with her last night, I thought maybe . . ." her voice trailed off, and she turned again to go, but Warbucks caught hold of her hand.

"Wait," he begged. He, too, had been remembering last night; how she'd cried at the film, how the two of them had put a sleeping child to bed. And there was something different about her today, something softer. He wasn't sure, but he thought it had something to do with her hair. Annie was right, he never noticed anything. But he could learn, couldn't he?

He drew Grace back into the chair beside him. "I just noticed something," he told her softly. "You're very pretty when you argue with me."

Twin spots of color appeared in Grace's creamy cheeks. "Thank you, sir, but—"

"Oliver."

"Oliver," she whispered, her eyes unable to meet his. Then she looked him full in the face. "Do you really love only money and power and capitalism?" He still had hold of her hand, and now Grace put her other little hand on top of his. "They're never going to love you back."

They were gazing now into each other's eyes, fascinated by what each saw in the other's depths. As with that first Garden at the beginning of recorded time, this one too held a man and a woman who were suddenly and passionately aware of one another.

"Your teeth are crooked," said Oliver in a near whisper.

"I'll have them fixed," blushed Grace.

"I like them crooked."

"I'll leave them."

"Thank you."

Without taking her eyes off his, Grace murmured, "I could get the papers signed this morning."

"Grace?"

"Oliver?"

"It means a great deal to you?"

The girl nodded. "A great deal."

"Then I'll do it myself," he decided. It was an enormous step for him to take, a man whose responsibilities were great but impersonal, a man who involved himself in everything but who was truly involved in nothing. And he never did anything in half measures. If Annie was to be his ward, she would be his to protect and defend and, yes, love.

Because he was coming to care for her a little. He could see her face as though she were standing in front of him this very minute. The eyes, so blue and honest; she was forthright and said exactly what she meant without fear. The red hair, sign of a feisty temper and a pair of fists to be wary of. That incredibly optimistic grin of hers, and the way she never let you see anything but the bright side of her. Why, she was like him in so many ways. And, in the ways they were different from each other, little Annie was the better person of the two, and he could learn from her. Yes, he loved Annie! She had, with her courage, and her independence, and her strength and intelligence, touched something in him that had never been open to touch before, something vital that had been close to dying undiscerned. She held his heart in her two little hands, and she was going to be his little girl.

A great happiness washed over Oliver Warbucks, and no day had ever been sunnier or more beautiful. In a few short moments he had found love, not in one place but two! What man had ever been happier?

"Oh, Mr. Warbucks, I could just kiss you!" cried Grace, and her lips were dangerously close to his. He reached for that kiss, but she'd already jumped up, her face radiant with a joy that matched his own. Never had he imagined she could be so beautiful, but then never had he imagined anything about her at all. It had taken Annie to bring the two of them together. No, it would be the three of them together.

Grace was running toward the house, to wake up Annie.

"Grace!" he called after her, and she stopped and turned, the sunlight illuminating her hair and making it glow.

"Get her a little present!"

"Oh, yes, Oliver!"

He thought for a second. "Something from Tiffany. A new locket."

Her eyes misted at his thoughtfulness. She, too, had been touched by the pathetic quality of the little broken locket Annie refused to take off. She'd buy her one a thousand times better. "Oh, Oliver!" she breathed. Then, as he reached her side, loping up the velvet lawn like a boy, she warned him with mock severity. "And you. Be careful when you go to the orphanage. That woman has claws and fangs."

He threw back his head and laughed, and Grace marveled at the rich sound of it. She realized she'd never heard him laugh before, and she was very grateful to Annie.

And then, surprised, she was in his arms, and being very thoroughly kissed by a billionaire, a mover and shaker of nations' destinies. He kissed exactly like a man.

Miss Hannigan woke up early, with a smile on her face. She'd been having a lovely dream. She dreamed that Annie was back from the Warbucks house, and scrubbing the floor in an evening gown, which was getting more and more dirty and torn the more she scrubbed. She dreamed that Annie had splinters in her fingers and scabs on her knees from the filthy old floor, and that, while the other orphans crowded around for their bowl of midday mush, Annie was forced to clean the chimneys, shinnying up them like a little monkey, and coming down all covered in soot and ashes, gasping, wheezing, and choking. And when she woke up, the smile on Miss Hannigan's face grew broader and brighter. Because the dream was going to come true. Today was the day.

She was so tickled that she was almost nice to some of the orphans today, but she caught herself in time, and forced herself to be extra nasty, to keep in practice for when Annie came back. She rather imagined it would be late in the day, because she was sure that trouble-making brat would stay to the last possible minute. *I know I would,* said Miss Hannigan.

So she was surprised to hear a powerful motor car drive up so early, but she hastened to the door, eager to get her meathooks on Annie in the first possible minute. She expected the Town Car and Miss Farrell, so she almost fainted at the peephole when she laid eyes on the gleaming, sporty Dusenberg and saw Oliver Warbucks step out.

It was unmistakably Oliver Warbucks. Not only had she seen his picture in the Sunday supplements time without number, but who else possessed that powerful posture, that commanding walk, that bald head, that diamond as big as a golf ball in his shirt front, that nine-foot-tall Indian bodyguard?

Nine-foot-tall Indian bodyguard? Was she still dreaming? No, there he was, standing watch on the pavement as Warbucks gave the bell an extra loud ring. There was no sign of Annie.

She flung the door wide.

"Good morning, Miss Hannigan," said Warbucks, brushing past her to the step inside.

"Holy Hannah," she whimpered as she caught the aroma of money and power that exuded from Warbucks. She followed after him like a hungry hound as he made his way down the corridors of the orphanage. He was shocked at the conditions that were evident to even a cursory glance, and he made some mental notes for immediate relief.

"I want to talk to you about Annie," he snapped, as he led the way into Miss Hannigan's office.

"You want to return her and forget it or you want to trade up?"

Warbucks opened his crocodile briefcase and pulled out an official-looking sheaf of papers. "I want to adopt her."

Miss Hannigan nodded slightly, and her expression didn't change. "Would you excuse me for just one moment?" she asked politely, and, at Warbucks' nod, she stepped into the supply closet and closed the door behind her. There she let out a blood-curdling scream, a Comanche yell of anger and frustration. Then, wiping her mouth with her pocket handkerchief, she stepped out smiling to confront the bewildered Warbucks.

"Thank you so much. Won't you please sit down?"

Oliver Warbucks placed the papers squarely on the desk in front of Miss Hannigan, then carefully seated himself and took a pen from the pocket of his coat. He looked up to see Miss Hannigan flaring her nostrils at him, her false eyelashes fluttering like moth wings.

"For a Republican you're sinfully handsome. Has anyone ever told you that?" She leaned forward like a snake, and her hands were suddenly all over him, fingering the expensive cloth of his Saville Row suit.

"Miss Hannigan—" began Warbucks in protest, but she was now focusing in on his stickpin, a single flawless diamond the size of a hen's egg.

"Oh, my gawd, is that thing real?" she breathed, regarding the stone with genuine lust.

"Just sign the papers," snapped Warbucks.

"What's it worth to you?"

Warbucks blinked in surprise. Miss Hannigan leaned back in her desk chair, regarding him through slitted eyes. She was breathing hard and beginning to tremble.

Oliver's face hardened. "What exactly do you mean, what's it worth to me?" he demanded coldly.

Miss Hannigan was now making kissing motions with her lips, looking like a carp in heat. "I go positively weak in the knees with men like you," she husked.

"Annie's told me a lot about your operation here."

"Misses me, huh?" sneered Hannigan.

"Clean sheets once a month, no schooling, no meat, no fresh vegetables or fruit," enumerated Warbucks in a voice of steel. "You're breaking every child welfare law on the books—"

"Would you care for a drink, my little billiard ball?" she invited, ignoring his anger and impatience.

Miss Hannigan stood up a bit unsteadily, and Warbucks stood, too, picking up the sheaf of adoption papers and waving them under her nose. She evaded them and danced into her adjacent apartment, Warbucks one step behind her. She knew that she had the power to divert, if she could only get him to stop talking about that adoption! Slinking like a snake from a silent movie, she made her way toward him, a scarf thrown over her shoulders, only to be met by the barrier of the papers and the pen.

"Sign," he commanded.

"In a moment, *chéri*. First, we have ze little drink, *non?*"

She whirled gracefully (she thought) into her other
room, and dipped two chipped tumblers bringing them up
brimming. When she popped back through the beaded curtains, he was still holding that pen and those papers, and
he waved the gin away in distaste.

"Sign."

"Oh, but, Oliver," she simpered in a Dixie drawl, "surely
there are more things for a man and a woman to talk
about than silly old papers?"

"SIGN."

That didn't work, French didn't work, and now southern
belle didn't work. Any one else would have fallen victim
to her persuasions long ago.

"Miss Hannigan, do you want to keep your job?"

"Not if there's an alternative," she said.

"The alternative is the streets," he told her coldly,
handing her the pen and the papers.

She snatched the pen from his fingers and furiously
scribbled her signature on the dotted line. "If that's the
way you feel about it, why didn't you say so in the first
place?"

Then she made one more try. "Now that I've signed,
would you care to celebrate?"

But Warbucks was already on his way to the door, the
precious adoption papers safe in his briefcase.

Miss Hannigan was so brought down by the events of
the morning, which had turned out so differently from
her hopes and dreams, that nothing could restore her to
her customary wonderful disposition except several tumblers of gin, taken directly from the tub. Thus fortified,
she stormed out of her office to exact vengeance from the
remaining orphans—and marched straight into the dead
mouse that Duffy was dangling. After shrieking her head
off for a full minute, Miss Hannigan clutched at her heart
and staggered back for another drink. The next time she
opened her office door, she did so with extreme caution,
one inch at a time. Satisfied that the rodent had vanished
(she would find it again, hours later, underneath her pillow), she made her way into the orphans' quarters.

"No lazing about, my little pig droppings, no luxury and

idleness for you. Industry! I want to see those drops of sweat flying, or it's kill! kill! kill!"

If she couldn't make Annie pay, she'd take it out of the hides of the others. Most especially, out of the hides of Annie's friends.

CHAPTER EIGHT

When Oliver Warbucks arrived home, he went directly to his gold and black marble bathroom, where he turned the shower on as hot as he could stand it and climbed under. He scrubbed at his skin for more than ten minutes, until he could feel clean again. It seemed to him that the dirt and the stench of the orphanage was still clinging to him, but it was the moral stench he was trying to wash away, the filth of Miss Hannigan's mind. He shuddered to think that he had come within a hair's breadth of sending Annie back to that horrible place. How right Grace had been! And how glad he was that today she looked so beautiful and so lovable that he could deny her nothing.

Well, never mind. Annie was soon going to be his daughter; he promised himself to give Grace Farrell a whopping raise and think about marrying her someday, and meanwhile all of them would go on happily together under one roof, as they'd done all week. Must remember to contact the board of orphans about Miss Hannigan. The woman is a monster, he mused, making mental notes. She ought not to be allowed within ten miles of helpless children.

After he dried himself, he selected a fresh set of clothing from the multitudes—all identical—that thronged his dressing room with its custom-built closets. Dressed and feeling somewhat refreshed, he repaired not to the office but to the grandeur of the drawing room, where a fire was lit in the fireplace, and gargantuan bouquets of roses and white lilac stood on the mantel and on the white piano. He sent for Grace, only to be told that she had not yet returned from her errand.

This information set his teeth on edge; he was as jumpy as a cat in a lightning storm. He began to pace the room, a caged animal smoking cigars, until the soles of his shoes had worn discernible ruts in the Axminster carpet's luxurious pile.

"Women!" he snorted to Punjab, who stood on the alert at the side of the fireplace nearest the door. "Does it take this long to get to Tiffany and back? Where is she?"

Punjab remained his usual unflappable self. "I hear the car, sahib," he remarked quietly.

"It's probably not the right car," fumed Warbucks.

"It's the Town Car. Miss Farrell took the Town Car."

A moment later, Grace rushed in, out of breath and looking lovely, a little blue box tied in a white bow conspicuous in her hands.

"What took you so long?" demanded Warbucks. "The Asp was due back with Annie ten minutes ago—" He whirled to Punjab. "Has something happened to *them?*"

The ghost of a smile crossed Punjab's face, but didn't land there. "They are in the kitchen, sahib."

Grace crossed to the fireplace and pulled the bellrope hanging there. A faint tinkle sounded in the kitchen below.

"I told the Asp to wait until I got back with this," she said, holding the Tiffany box out to Oliver.

He snatched it from her fingers. "Why doesn't anyone tell me anything?" he pouted.

"Mr. Warbucks," said Grace, declining to use his Christian name in front of Punjab, "there's no need to be nervous."

"Nervous? Who's nervous?" squeaked Warbucks nervously. "Do I look nervous to you?" he demanded of Punjab. "Do I look nervous to you?" he asked Grace rhetorically. He whirled to confront himself in the mirror. "Do I look nervous? No. Do I look warm and loving? No." His face fell. He thrust the blue box back into Grace's hands. "You give it to her," he pleaded.

But Grace was handing the box back, Grace was shaking her head no.

"It was your idea, sir . . ." she reminded him.

Warbucks pushed the box back at her again. "She likes you better than she likes me."

Grace allowed herself the luxury of a smile. "Oliver, pull yourself together," she admonished him. It tickled her that this man, who was the equal of potentates and princes, who dealt daily with ambassadors, papal legates, and presidents, should come unglued at the thought of giving a little gold locket to a ten-year-old orphan.

It was at that moment that Annie skipped in, followed by the Asp and Sandy, still skidding on the waxed surfaces of the hallway floor. Since nobody had appeared to be around when Annie woke up that day, and nobody had said anything to her about what time she was due back on Hudson Street, Annie had stuck to her usual schedule. This included her karate lesson with the Asp, and she was wearing the pajamalike karate suit when she came running into the living room.

"Oh, Mr. Warbucks! Wanna see what the Asp taught me today?"

Before Oliver could answer, Annie struck out with her left foot, catching Warbucks on the kneecap and sending him hurtling to the ground in agony.

As Punjab and the Asp rushed forward to raise their fallen master, Annie's face went white and she threw herself down beside Warbucks, her features contorted in sorrow.

"Oh, gee, I didn't think it would work!" she gasped.

"To the couch, Punjab, if you don't mind," said Mr. Warbucks through gritted teeth. As Punjab stretched the billionaire out gently, and began to palpate the injured leg, Warbucks called out to the angry and humiliated Asp.

"It's all right, Asp. Now she knows it works. I believe in being able to defend yourself. Even for girls."

"Shall I call the doctor, sahib?" asked Punjab.

"No, fix it yourself," instructed his master. As the Indian giant made some mystical passes in the air over Warbucks' knee, Oliver felt the pain beginning to leave him. After less than a minute, he announced, "The pain is gone. I'm fine now."

Annie and Grace breathed audible sighs of relief. When the Asp and Punjab had rushed to the aid of Warbucks, Grace, knowing that she'd only be in the way and knowing, too, that Annie needed her, had stood close to the little girl, holding her by the shoulders and giving her little hugs for comfort. Now she stepped forward and laid the little blue box on Oliver's chest, next to his hands.

"We'll leave you alone a moment," she said.

Warbucks gave her an imploring look from panicked eyes, but Grace merely nodded to the Asp and Punjab, who followed her out of the room. Annie and Mr. Warbucks were alone.

Feeling like an awkward schoolboy, Oliver slipped the Tiffany box into his pocket and took Annie by the hand. He wasn't sure how to begin, so the two of them sat there for a minute or so in silence. Then Warbucks said, "Annie, I want to talk to you about something very serious."

Annie bit her lip. "You don't want me anymore, right?" she said as cheerfully as she could through the pain in her heart.

This caught Warbucks totally off balance. "On the contrary . . . I *do* . . . good Lord . . ."

They sat for a minute more in silence, Annie searching her memory for something she might have done to offend Mr. Warbucks. It must be serious or he wouldn't be looking so uncomfortable. Or maybe it was just that, because this was to be her last day, Mr. Warbucks wanted to give her a useful little lecture on life to take back with her to the orphanage. Whatever it was, it didn't look as though it was going to be pleasant for either of them.

"Annie, can we have a man-to-man talk?" asked Warbucks at last.

Uh-oh, thought Annie. Out loud, she said, "Sure."

But still he couldn't meet her eyes, or find an appropriate jumping-off point. He didn't want to tell her too much; there was more brimming inside him than Annie needed to deal with, but he didn't want to tell her too little either. He wanted for both of them to live happily ever after, nothing more nor less. And that wasn't going to be as easy as it sounded.

He took a deep breath and went for it. "What I'm proposing would involve a long-term . . . well . . . agreement."

Bewildered, Annie could only stare at him. She hadn't the faintest idea of what he was driving at.

This sitting still was driving Warbucks crazy. He stood up and began pacing back and forth.

"Actually, maybe you should know more about me before you make up your mind," he told her.

"Okay," agreed Annie readily. She still had no idea

what he was talking about, but whatever it was, it was making Mr. Warbucks sweat, and she'd never seen him sweat, not even when he was on the telephone yelling at Mussolini.

"Let's go for a walk," he suggested. What he needed was a breath of air.

"Okay," said Annie, standing up immediately.

As soon as they reached the back garden through the kitchen door, Oliver Warbucks let his breath out in a deep sigh of relief. This was better, much better. He began to tell Annie about himself. "I was born in Liverpool, in a railroad switch house," he began. *Ah,* she thought, *England. That's why he has that strange accent.*

"My brother died of pneumonia because we didn't have the money for medicine. Well, I decided then and there one day I would be rich. Very, very rich."

"Good idea," Annie agreed. But it was difficult for her to picture Oliver Warbucks either as very young or very poor.

The back garden was terraced, and old stone steps, covered in picturesque silvery moss, led down to a small pool, a stone bench and some very old trees. Side by side, they walked down the steps. Warbucks strode with his hands clasped behind his back, and Annie was a step or two behind him, her hands clasped the same way in unconscious imitation of him. Sandy pattered along at his mistress's side, just happy to be out in this beautiful weather with a full belly and Annie by his side. He had achieved canine Nirvana, and wouldn't have traded his lot for that of the most pampered Pekinese lapdog.

"In those days," continued Mr. Warbucks, "America was the land of opportunity. I signed on a ship as cabin boy when I was twelve. By the time I was twenty-one, I'd made my first million. In the next ten years, I turned that into a hundred million." He stopped and turned to Annie, waiting for her reaction.

"Wow!" What else was there to say? Annie could no more conceive of what a hundred million dollars was like than she could flap her wings and take off.

"In those days, that was a lot of money," added Warbucks, and Annie nodded her concurrence. It sure was.

"I was ruthless, hurt a lot of people. But, like the man

94

says, you don't have to be nice to the people you meet on the way up if you're not coming back down. Making money was all I ever cared about." He paused, then added softly, "Until now." He looked significantly at Annie, but she was still in the dark. Even so, she was enjoying this walk and talk, and she gave Oliver Warbucks a heartfelt smile.

He fingered the little box in his pocket. "Let's go inside," he said abruptly.

"Okay," said Annie agreeably.

Once back in the monumental living room, Warbucks resumed his pacing, while Annie sat in a baronial red-velvet chair, trying to follow what he was saying.

"It's occurred to me that no matter how much money I have, no matter how many houses, how many Rembrandts and Dusenbergs, if I have no one to . . . share it with, well, I might as well be back in Liverpool, broke." He turned to her, stopping in his tracks. "Annie, do you understand what I'm trying to say?" he demanded.

"Sure," said Annie uncertainly. Did it have something to do with Grace Farrell? Annie kind of suspected it might, but then why was Mr. Warbucks talking to *her* and not to Grace?

"Good," said Warbucks, straightening up and letting his breath out.

"Kind of," Annie added, rather timidly for her.

"Kind of?"

"I guess not," she admitted. She was letting Mr. Warbucks down, and she knew it, and it embarrassed her.

Here they were, back on square one. Well, there was ony one more thing he could think of to do. He took the little blue box from Tiffany out of his pocket and shoved it into Annie's hands. Taken totally by surprise, she looked up at him, bewildered.

"You've given me so much already, Mr. Warbucks," she protested.

Warbucks beamed at her. "I got the papers signed today. It's official."

Annie was busy untying the ribbon on the box.

"What is?" she asked, and then she saw the locket, and a strange expression came over her face. "It's so pretty, but . . ."

95

Warbucks, watching her lift the little gold locket out of the cotton-lined box, noticed neither the expression on her face nor the "but." He took it out of her hands and undid the clasp himself.

"Here, let me put it on you," he said gently, but Annie broke away from him and ran, shouting "No!" fiercely.

At her shout, the household staff and Grace, who'd been waiting outside with their congratulations, ran in, concerned.

But Annie and Warbucks didn't even see them; they were staring at each other, pain written on both their faces.

"It's a really swell locket, Mr. Warbucks, but if it's all the same to you, I'll keep my old one." Tears were beginning to form behind her eyes, and she blinked them back ferociously. She could see that she'd hurt Mr. Warbucks, and she could kick herself for that, but it couldn't be helped.

Warbucks was hurt beyond anything Annie could comprehend. He had never for one minute anticipated that the scene could be played this way.

"It's *not* all the same to me," he retorted angrily. "Your old one's broken. This one's engraved. You didn't even look at it." He turned the locket over in his hand and read the pretty script on the back. " 'To Annie, with love from . . . "Daddy" Warbucks.' " He glared at Grace. Daddy? Wasn't that carrying things a bit far?

Didn't anybody understand? Annie looked around her for support, but it was evident that everybody in the room thought she was being ungrateful; their sympathies were with Mr. Warbucks. Suddenly, it burst on her—what all of this was about. What the words on the locket meant. What Mr. Warbucks had been trying to tell her with so much difficulty. He wanted to adopt her, that's what those papers meant. He wanted her to be his little girl. No wonder he was so hurt. But how was he to know? She hadn't told any of them about the Dream.

Now she was going to have to hurt him even more. Because, although she liked him so much . . . no, *loved* him . . . she couldn't be his adopted daughter. Annie drew a deep breath.

"Mr. Warbucks, when my folks left me at the orphanage ten years ago, they left a note saying they'd come back to get me, soon as they could, and that they'd keep the other half of this old locket, so I'd know them when they came."

She paused, and she heard a murmur of astonishment from the staff, spreading like a ripple. Only Mr. Warbucks and Grace Farrell said nothing. Grace kept looking from Annie to Oliver and back again, hurting for both of them at once.

"I'm gonna find them someday, Mr. Warbucks," Annie continued in a softer voice. "I'm gonna have a regular mother and father like a regular kid. I am."

Hearing these words, Oliver Warbucks felt the heart break in his chest, although his anger disappeared. He'd never expected this, that Annie would say no. That she had a reason to say no. He'd had a rosy vision of the four of them walking down life's pathway together, Annie and Warbucks and Grace and even that dog of Annie's. And here he was, the richest and most powerful man in the world, savior of nations, on the brink of tears because a little orphan girl had turned him down! He'd had absolutely no idea of how much he'd come to love her until this minute, when she was telling him gently that he couldn't be her "Daddy" because she already had a Daddy somewhere.

And yet, he felt closer to her now than ever before, because he could hear the pain and determination in her words, and they reminded him so much of the boy he'd been, back in England long ago, when he'd vowed that he would be very, very rich.

"I don't mean to hurt your feelings," Annie said, choking back her own tears. "You've been nicer to me than anybody in the whole wide world. But I been dreaming of my folks for as long as I can remember, and I just gotta find them." She stopped, having said everything she could.

It took him a silent minute, but Oliver Warbucks pulled himself together. Then he formed a resolve. By thunder, he wasn't the most powerful man in the world for nothing! If Annie wanted her parents, Annie would get her parents. He, Oliver Warbucks the billionaire, would see to it personally. Now he was on firm ground, on turf that he owned and operated, and he began to bark orders at everybody.

"Well then, I'll help you." He turned to Drake. "Get me J. Edgar Hoover on the phone." To Grace, he said, "Get me Mayor LaGuardia and the chief of police." At the Asp, he growled, "Get me Walter Winchell," and to Punjab, "Get me Lowell Thomas."

Everyone scattered, scurrying off to do his bidding.

They were alone again, Warbucks and Annie. They looked at each other with love, but Warbucks wasn't going to soften again. "And you," he said to the little girl, "when we get all this under way, I'll take *you* to Washington!"

This was more happiness than Annie could hold; it was starting to spill over and roll down her cheeks in the form of tears. To have a mother and a father! She knew Oliver Warbucks well enough to know that if anybody on the face of the planet could find them for her, it was him. And now, to meet the president, her hero. Her *other* hero, she corrected herself. Well, she just wanted to go off somewhere and blubber for joy, with only Sandy to see her. Darting forward, she threw her arms around Oliver Warbucks' neck and gave him a swift, loving hug. Then she ran out, Sandy at her heels, and vanished up to her room.

Warbucks stood looking after Annie. Ironic, he needed her more than she needed him! Who would ever have guessed it? Well, at least he could do this one thing for her. He looked down. In his hand he was still holding the little gold locket from Tiffany. For a moment, his fingers closed around it tightly, as though to crush it, the tangible symbol of his greatest disappointment. Then he sighed, and dropped it into his pocket. No time for wasteful and useless sentimentality. Not when there was work to be done.

CHAPTER NINE

Today, television brings the entire world into your living room, with nightly news to tell you how many disasters have taken place all in one day. In 1933, people had the same dependence on the radio. Radio brought them everything—music, comedy, drama, true stories, mysteries, the news, the weather, and the racing results. In the evenings, people sat around and *watched* radio. They gathered around the box as though it were some kind of holy temple, and looked at the sounds coming out of it. If you were a big star in the movies or on stage, you went into radio. If you were a top singer, radio was the place for you. More people heard you on the air than ever went out to buy your records.

Walter Winchell was the number-one columnist of his day, but he got bigger when he went on the air to broadcast to "Mr. and Mrs. America and all the ships at sea." Radio reached everybody, rich and poor, black and white, young and old. It even reached the orphans at the Hudson Street Home for Girls, Established 1891. That was no thanks to Miss Hannigan, who owned the only radio in the building, and who was addicted to daytime soap operas (yes, they started on the radio) like "Young Widder Brown," "The Romance of Helen Trent," "Our Gal Sunday," "Mary Noble, Backstage Wife," "Aunt Jenny's Real Life Stories," "Lorenzo Jones," and "Pepper Young's Family."

The orphans had worked out a system for gaining access to the precious radio. The best time was when Miss Hannigan was asleep. (I told you she had her good side.) Then,

99

they simply tiptoed in and snaffled it, carrying it off (it was a table model) to a room with a closed door and playing it very quietly. It was then they learned all the new songs, such as "Oh, You Nasty Man" and "I'll Be Glad When You're Dead, You Rascal You," which they dedicated to Miss Hannigan.

But Miss Hannigan didn't always oblige by sleeping, so the orphans sometimes turned to Plan B. This involved taking turns, three at a time, with two girls getting to listen, and one to stand guard. There was a small hole in the wall of Miss Hannigan's bedroom, which led to the outer corridor, and by dint of much scraping, Pepper and Duffy had enlarged the hole enough to be able to hear most of what was being broadcast. Faintly, but it served the purpose. The two lucky girls whose turn it was would bring mops and pails with them, so that if Miss Hannigan emerged suddenly, as was her happy custom, yelling "Kill! kill! kill!" the girl on guard would whistle a warning, and all Miss Hannigan would see were two diligent orphans scrubbing the corridor outside her room.

Miss Hannigan listened to the radio all the time. The romance-dramas and the soaps were her favorites; they always put her in a miserable mood, which she relieved by taking it out on the orphans. But actually, she'd listen to anything, even the Iodent Toothpaste Hour, an awful melange of bad music and bad comedy, therefore everybody's favorite program. The Iodent Toothpaste Hour starred the inevitable M.C., a trio of dreadful girl singers who dressed like triplets, and a comedy team comprising a ventriloquist named McKracky and his dummy, Wacky, very bad imitations of Edgar Bergen and Charlie McCarthy. Miss Hannigan loved the program and never missed it.

She was listening to it tonight. Miss Hannigan had fallen on hard times in the last few days. She had been forced to face the prospect of her least favorite orphan, that miserable troublemaker and rotten kid, falling into the gravy boat.

Was it any wonder that her only consolation in life was the radio? She had it turned on right now, listening to the Iodent Toothpaste Hour, as most of America was doing.

Bert Healy, the M.C., had promised his listening audience a big surprise, a real-life heartwarming human drama, guaranteed to bring a lump to the throat and a tear to the eye. Miss Hannigan dearly loved a good cry; she was blessed with so tender a heart. So she was listening eagerly when Healy announced, in his oleaginous broadcaster's tones:

"I'd like to introduce a little orphan named Annie."

A little orphan named Annie? Could there be two? Impossible! So Miss Hannigan did the only thing possible in the circumstances. She screamed and fainted.

Well, wouldn't you? She tumbled straight down, and her head hit the bathroom floor hard enough to knock her out.

The two orphans out in the hall, at the earhole, were Molly and Pepper. When Molly heard Annie's name, she, too, jumped up and screamed, but she didn't faint. She was too eager to find out what was going to happen next.

Just as today the parents of a missing child might go on television to plead for his return, so Oliver Warbucks decided that, to reach the most people in the quickest way, he must take Annie's case to the radio audience in the forty-eight states. Of course, his first idea was the news broadcast. It was timely and above all it was dignified, as befitted a billionaire and something of a newsmaker himself.

But Oliver was soon convinced that nobody listened to the news. On the other hand, just about everybody in America listened to the Iodent Toothpaste Hour, and Annie's real father and mother might very well be among them. Certainly, it was worth a try.

So Warbucks had Grace telephone the head of the Red Network (nothing to do with the Bolsheviks; there were two radio networks in those days, the Red and the Blue, which later evolved into the CBS and NBC we know and revere today). The head of the Red Network notified the sponsors and the sponsors thought it wasn't quite the right thing for Iodent Toothpaste's image. So Oliver Warbucks bought the Iodent Toothpaste Company outright, and didn't have to listen to any more arguments. To the station they all of them went.

The top radio writers in the business had knocked out a quick script. Time was of the essence; once Oliver Warbucks had made his mind up he wanted to see immediate results from the decision. When they arrived at the radio broadcasting studio, they were handed the pages of the script and told where to stand.

Annie was surprised. Here she'd been listening to the Iodent Toothpaste Hour for years, and she'd pictured it very differently. Somehow she'd imagined a big stage and a real show going on. Instead, it was a really small studio, with four floor microphones—one for Bert Healy; one for McKracky and Wacky; one for the girl singers, the Lovely and Famous Moylan Sisters, Tilly, Milly and Agnes; and one for the most important person on the program, the sound effects man. There was a huge clock on the wall with a long sweep second hand, a little sign that lit up and said On the Air when they were on the air, and a soundproof control booth with dials and knobs to twist, in which sat the producer of the program wearing headphones. He communicated with his cast by making menacing faces and threatening gestures through the glass.

Annie and Mr. Warbucks were to share Bert Healy's mike. Oliver had never used a live mike before, although he was quite used to dictating, and had not laid eyes on the script until this very second. Otherwise, they were prepared.

At last the sweep second hand came around to the hour, and the sound man put the opening theme song on the record player. Bert Healy cried with great enthusiasm, "Good evening, ladies and gentlemen, it's the Iodent Toothpaste Hour!" and the sound effects man turned on the applause machine, which simulated a large audience breaking into wild and spontaneous applause. Then the sound man opened a door, and walked two shoes with leather heels over a wooden board. Footsteps. Annie was fascinated.

" 'Say,' " Wacky McKracky, the ventriloquist's dummy,

said into his mike, pretending to read it off the script, " 'who's that who just walked into our Red Network station, Bert Healy?' "

Healy stepped to his mike and read, " 'Wacky, it's none other than the Wall Street tycoon, Oliver Warbucks!' "

More applause, long and loud, from the machine.

Silence from Warbucks, until the assistant director pointed frantically to the place on Warbucks' script where he was supposed to start.

" 'Thank you, Bert Healy,' " read Oliver slowly. " 'It's swell' "—he looked up scowling; "swell?" he queried with disdain—" 'to be on the Iodent Hour.' "

" 'I understand,' " read Healy, picking up the tempo, " 'that you're conducting a coast-to-coast search for Annie's parents.' "

Warbucks nodded, a gesture entirely lost on a radio audience. The assistant director darted forward again, his finger on the script.

" 'Yes. Bert Healy, I am now conducting a coast-to-coast nationwide search for Annie's parents. Drop page.' "

He looked up, mystified. Drop page? Then he noticed the other radio actors dropping their script pages on the studio floor as they finished them, and he understood. Paper rattles, especially in front of a live microphone, so radio people drop their finished pages silently instead of tucking them behind the others.

Oliver nodded and continued. " 'Warbucks,' " he read, once again including the stage directions, " 'Furthermore, tonight I am offering a cash reward to Annie's parents. Fifty thousand dollars. Cash.' "

This was the first time Annie had heard anything of the reward money, and the announcement filled her with excitement. Dropping her script, she ran to Oliver and embraced him, hugging him tightly.

"Are you really? Oh, Mr. Warbucks, you are the wonderfullest man in the whole wide world." And that's how it went out over the air.

Miss Hannigan, unfortunately for her, had come to in time to hear Warbucks' offer and Annie's spontaneous reaction. It almost made her sick; it was a good thing she was already in the bathroom. Her head was beginning to ache from the grinding of her molars; God was really picking on her lately. Fifty thousand dollars!

Outside, the orphans had their ears pressed up to the office wall, listening to Bert Healy saying:

" 'So, if you're listening, Annie's parents, contact Oliver Warbucks—' "

" 'Warbucks. Interrupts,' " interrupted Oliver Warbucks, reading off the paper. " 'At my house. 987 Fifth Avenue, New York City.' "

Molly leaped to her feet, her brown eyes huge with excitement. "Annie's gonna find her folks!" she yelled.

Miss Hannigan, hearing the same announcement, winced.

In the studio, Mr. Warbucks was down to his last sheet of script. By now, he was a master at the mike, and spoke with booming confidence, causing the sound-level dials to spin like roulette wheels in the control booth, and the producer to tear his hair out.

" 'Thank you, Bert Healy, and thank you, Iodent Toothpaste, with the all-new miracle ingredient, Y-37, to fight bad breath, for letting me come and talk to you this evening. Good night, Bert Healy, and good night for the Red Network. Drop page.' "

He dropped the page and strode angrily toward the studio exit, furious for allowing himself to be suckered into doing a commercial for bad breath. He made a mental note to buy the Red Network and fire Bert Healy and everybody connected with the Iodent Toothpaste Hour.

Behind him, the sound effects man turned the volume up up up on the applause.

The announcement caused as much joy among the orphans as it did pain to Miss Hannigan. The story spread like wildfire from dormitory to dormitory, until every girl in the Hudson Street Home knew that Annie was going to find her parents, and that Mr. Warbucks, the billionaire, was going to pay out a hundred million dollars to whoever was Annie's mother and father. What a sock in the eye to Hannigan! What a kick in the teeth! What a pain in the you-know-where! And what a boost for the orphans! It would put them on the map, for certain sure. And who knows? Maybe a slew of would-be mothers and fathers would turn up at the Hudson Street Home looking for little girls to adopt, in case some other billionaire might be handing out mazuma.

Miss Hannigan had been dealt some severe body blows one right after the other, but tonight was the knockout punch. Fifty thousand American dollars were to be laid out to find a happy ending for that little redheaded brat, while she, Loretta Louise Mary Margaret Hannigan, was still wearing her lovely feminine fingers down to the bone nursing and caring for an ungrateful, undeserving, undermining passel of low-life orphans, all of whom put together weren't worth fifty American cents. Was there no justice in the world? Up there, somewhere, she could hear the sounds of godly laughter. What fools these Hannigans be! No, by all that was unholy, the ghostly laughter was not from up there, but from out *here*—right outside her door. The final indignity, the straw that put the camel's sacroiliac out of whack! Oh, what she wouldn't give for the mask of Medusa to turn these orphans to stone! Laughing! I'll show them laughing!

She threw open the door, and the orphans froze. They'd seen her mad, they'd seen her drunk, they'd seen her crazy. But they had never seen Miss Hannigan so mad drunk crazy as she was at this very moment in time. It frightened them.

"Did I hear happiness in here?" she shrieked. *"Did I hear sounds of merriment and mirth? Did my ears detect joy?"*

The girls scattered in all directions, fleeing for their lives, while Miss Hannigan's "Kill! kill! kill!" echoed to the skies and the street. And heaven help the laggard orphan who couldn't keep up. Miss Hannigan would have her scrubbing down the attic ceiling at four in the morning.

Like all media events, the story of the orphan girl Annie, as the press called it, was on everybody's lips the following day. Right after the broadcast, the mansion had been besieged by reporters and photographers from the major New York newspapers—the *Daily News,* the *Mirror,* the *Journal,* the *American,* the *Herald-Tribune,* the *Times, the Sun* and the *World. Life* and *Judge* and the *Police Gazette* sent photojournalists; the *New Yorker* sent Dorothy Parker; and *Vanity Fair* dispatched Cecil Beaton to take pictures. Adela Rogers St. John came as a free lance. Warbucks received them all graciously, plied them with food and drink, and Annie told her story. With one big omission. Warbucks and Grace had instructed her carefully not to breathe syllable one about which orphanage she came from or about the locket. For, as they explained to her, how was she going to know if they would be her real folks unless she and they were the only ones to know where they'd left her or about the broken locket? Annie saw the reasoning behind it, and kept mum, telling only about the note. And Warbucks reiterated his offer, fifty thousand dollars to the couple who could prove they were Annie's parents.

What they also kept to themselves was the fact that Annie and Warbucks were heading out of town, nor did they tell the press where they were going.

Early the next morning, by prearrangement, Annie and Sandy met Oliver and Grace on the roof of the mansion. There the autocopter was kept, on what Warbucks called laughingly a "helipad." Annie was dressed in a leather coat and goggles, like a miniature fighter pilot. Warbucks had on what he always had on, a three-piece black suit, stiff collar, bow tie, and his outrageous diamond stickpin. He would show That Man how a Republican dressed.

As they climbed into the single seat of the autocopter (license plate NY-3, the Asp at the joystick), Grace ducked low to avoid the downdraft from the rotors, and backed off to wave them good-bye. Annie, who had never been up higher than the third floor, felt her stomach do tricks as the 'copter raised itself straight up, as though by Punjab's magic. The racket from the engine and the blades was terrible, but the view was magnificent. Below her was spread the entire Warbucks estate, and most of upper Fifth Avenue as well. And what was that long snaking line of people doing in front of the house? It was moving, stretching out for blocks down the avenue.

"Mr. Warbucks, look!"

Warbucks looked down. It was exactly as he'd feared. Hundreds and hundreds of couples were down there, lines of them beginning to form, pushing, shoving men and women, all determined to collect that fifty thousand dollars they'd heard about on the radio or read about in the papers. Annie and Warbucks were today's headlines, front-page stuff. And stealing the show was the fifty thousand smackers. And if they had to take in an orphan kid to collect, it made no never mind. How much can a ten-year-old kid eat? The mutt could always go to the pound.

Every couple on the jostling line was shouting out its own claims to be the real article, while deriding the claims of the others. There were couples with real red hair, and couples who'd gotten up extra early for a dye job. There were Irish couples and Spanish couples, Italian couples, Jewish couples, Polish, Ukrainian, even Chinese couples!

Annie, once Warbucks had explained the matter to her, was totally bewildered. She had only one mother and one father, right? That's all anybody ever *could* have for real. So who were all these other people and what did they want?

"Money, I'm afraid, Annie," said Mr. Warbucks as gently as he could.

Annie shook her head. They were willing to tell such a whopping lie for money! For the first time, she realized that finding her parents might not be all that simple and clear-cut. And another thought crept into her mind for the first time. Suppose they *did* turn up. Suppose they were down there right this minute, holding the other half of the broken locket that only she and they knew about? Well, where had they been before this? Why hadn't they come back for her at any time during the last ten years? How could she be sure that it was Annie and not the fifty thousand they were coming to get?

No, that was impossible. Times were bad, everybody knew that. There was a depression on, wasn't there? So it stood to reason that they'd been too poor to come and get her, but now the fifty thousand would enable them to buy her food and give her shelter. They'd be a family again. Mr. Warbucks must have known that would be the case; that's probably why he offered the money. The thought struck her again that he was the kindest person in the world, underneath all that power.

The cityscape had given way to the beaches and pine barrens of New Jersey as the 'copter headed due south to Washington, D.C., but back on upper Fifth Avenue, all was chaos. Punjab had opened the doors, and the line was supposed to proceed a couple at a time, with Grace Farrell asking the questions and taking the notes. But at the first sign of the massive wooden doors beginning to open, the wavering lines broke into a mob and everybody stormed the gates at once. Even Punjab was no match for the howling couples, who pushed their way in, trampling everything and everybody in their path, yelling for Annie and for the fifty thousand fish.

The scenery below the 'copter was spectacular, but Annie hardly saw it. She was thinking hard, and her little brow was knotted. She might be close now to having a family of her own, and it suddenly scared her. What would it be like not to be an orphan anymore? For the first time in many days, she thought about the Dream. What if her parents turned out to be nothing like the dream images she had of them? After all, why should they be? It was only a child's fantasy. Annie suddenly felt very alone. Anxiously, she turned to Oliver Warbucks and shouted over the racket of the 'copter.

"If all your dreams come true, do you die?"

Warbucks gave a shout of laughter and squeezed Annie's shoulder. "Of course not," he yelled in her ear, "you live happily ever after."

Annie laughed, suddenly relieved. She was being silly. Her parents were going to be wonderful, and they *would* live happily ever after. And Mr. Warbucks and Miss Farrell would always be her friends.

And meanwhile, in less than an hour she was going to meet the thirty-second president of the United States, Franklin Delano Roosevelt. And Eleanor, too.

CHAPTER TEN

The thirty-second president of the United States was just as eager to meet Annie as she was to meet him. After all, Annie (and the fifty thousand simoleons) had pushed him and his New Deal right off the front pages of every newspaper in the country. Which gave him at least one day of peace and quiet. FDR (and Eleanor, too) was curious to see the little redheaded orphan who had captured the nation's imagination. Besides, FDR was an extremely shrewd politician, and he knew that his leverage with Annie would be his leverage with Warbucks. It had not escaped the president's notice that this change of mind on Warbucks' part, to visit with him and talk with him, followed *after* Annie had come into the billionaire's life. Before that, Warbucks wouldn't even take his telephone calls.

The thing about politicians is that, no matter how honorable their objectives, no matter how high their moral tone or how outstanding their virtues, there's not one man jack of them who is above using a ten-year-old girl for political purposes if one floats within reach.

And now they were coming, and would stay to tea, and would be here, if the 'copter were on schedule, within the next fifteen minutes. With his handicap, and with the dignity of the highest office in the land, the president (and Eleanor, too) might have sat in state in the White House and waited for Warbucks to be ushered in. But FDR had the mind and heart of a small boy (even if his body had betrayed him) and he had heard a great deal about the potential military uses of the peculiar craft that Warbucks had developed, but had never seen one. He wasn't about to miss out on this opportunity. So, with Eleanor pushing his wheelchair, he set out down the White House lawn to watch the 'copter land.

There it was, right on time, puffing and chugging its lazy way across the sky. The machine still had to go back to the drawing board for speed, but what was outstanding about it was its maneuverability. Now, for instance, the Asp was sizing up the lawn as a place to land, and the 'copter's controls were in "hover." And hover it did, like the fattest hummingbird in the world, and the noisiest. And when it began to set down, it came down in a perfectly vertical approach.

"Marvelous!" laughed FDR, his cigarette holder pointing at the sky. "Aren't Republicans ostentatious?"

"Franklin, behave," his wife chided humorously. "It's astonishing that he's here at all."

The Asp brought the ship down in a perfect one-point landing, and switched off the rotors. But it took the blades time to come to a full stop, and they churned up a fearful wind, enough to snatch the president's yachting cap off his head and send it tumbling and skimming across the White House lawn. Two Secret Service men went barreling after it.

"What do you call this thing, Oliver?" shouted FDR over the wind, after Warbucks and Annie had climbed cautiously out of the craft.

"An autocopter," the billionaire shouted back. "You don't need an airport, just a backyard."

Suddenly shy now that she was really here, Annie ducked behind Oliver Warbucks.

The parties came together, and Warbucks bent to kiss the First Lady's hand with consummate gallantry.

"I appreciate your coming down here," said the president. "It means a great deal—"

"It means nothing," Warbucks interrupted sharply. "It means only that"—he reached around behind him and pulled Annie out—"Annie wanted to meet you."

Laughing, the president leaned forward in his wheelchair—which was an old office chair fitted out with a set of baby buggy tires, Annie was astonished to notice—and took Annie's hand, shaking it with great ceremony.

"It's nice to meet you, Mr. President Roosevelt," said Annie in the smallest voice of which she was capable.

"It's my pleasure, Annie." The president's eyes twinkled into Annie's own. "And thank you for bringing the old goat. We'll make a New Dealer of him yet."

Now it was Oliver Warbucks' turn to laugh. "Inconceivable!"

With his strong hands, the president turned his chair around and headed uphill toward the White House. Feeling a bit more at ease, Annie ran to help push it, smiling shyly at Mrs. Roosevelt, while the two men continued talking.

"If I can change Bernard Baruch's mind, I can change yours," said FDR.

Warbucks shook his head again, this time more firmly.

"Never," he said shortly, his Republican hackles rising.

"Don't mind him, Oliver," said Eleanor smoothly, taking his arm. She was often FDR's buffer, and did it graciously.

Annie was surprised to find the White House so modest, but then she was comparing it with the Warbucks mansion. Three decades later, another First Lady, Mrs. John F. Kennedy, would refurbish the old White House and make it sparkle, but on the day Annie visited it it was something on the shabby side, with worn carpets, threadbare furniture, and ancient draperies. Still, there was a sense of history in every room, a feeling of great events having taken place here, of the destinies of nations and peoples having been altered in these halls.

They had tea in the little drawing room outside FDR's office, and it was a pretty room, just like the living room in the Dream, comfortable, with soft places to sit.

They had a simple meal—fruit and cakes, cookies, and cups of tea and tiny sandwiches, and Annie helped pass the plates around. At first, only polite small talk was made, which gave Annie a chance to study the president and the First Lady. They looked very much like their pictures in the magazines and newspaper supplements she'd sneaked a peek at in Miss Hannigan's office back at the orphanage.

FDR had been a vigorous active man, a sailor, a sportsman, when he'd been struck down by a crippling disease, infantile paralysis, the dreaded poliomyelitis. It left him without the use of his legs, a cripple in a wheelchair.

But it hadn't taken away any of his dedication; if anything, it had strengthened his sense of purpose, and he had campaigned for and won the presidency of the United States from a wheelchair, an unheard-of victory. He had been a handsome man at one time; Annie could see the tattered remnants of that beauty still in his face, but the lively eyes were sunken in dark ringed sockets, and the famous jaw, jutting and proud, had wattles under the chin.

As for Anna Eleanor Roosevelt, the president's wife, well, she had never been a beauty to begin with and she wasn't a beauty now. Her face was on the horsey side, and her famous buck teeth had been caricatured by every Republican newspaper cartoonist in the country. But to Annie none of that mattered. She perceived in the First Lady an inner glow that transformed her features when she spoke, gave her an air of majesty. And Mrs. Roosevelt's eyes were truly beautiful, large, clear, warm, and kind. Annie felt at home right away.

But eventually the talk turned inevitably to politics, and there politeness gave ground to conviction.

Oliver Warbucks had been furious when FDR had closed the banks for federal inspection and given them a "holiday." It was against every business principle he held sacred. Even though it did give the banking institutions a short breathing space to recover and even though it forestalled another run on the banks, Warbucks disapproved mightily of the high-handed way that the president interfered in big business, and he'd set up a howl when Congress had voted FDR extraordinary powers.

He set up a howl now, too.

"The New Deal, in my opinion, is badly planned, badly organized, and badly administered. You don't think your programs through, Franklin, you don't think of what they're going to do to the economy in the long run."

"People don't eat in the long run," said the president mildly.

Mrs. Roosevelt put a protective arm around Annie. "Parents can't feed their children," she added.

"The lucky ones end up in orphanages," said FDR shrewdly, an unspoken reference to Annie.

"The older ones are abandoned, to steal, to starve—"

112

"The business of this country is business," Warbucks interrupted. "You should——"

"I want to put them to work," interrupted FDR in his turn.

Eleanor's lovely eyes were alight with enthusiasm.

"In the national parks, building camps, clearing trails, fighting fires, planting trees——"

"Hold it! Hold it!" protested Oliver, but FDR caught up the refrain.

"I want to feed them and house them and pay them. Not much but enough so they can send a little back to their parents, hold up their heads, and be proud to be Americans!"

Annie's eyes were shining, too. "That's a swell idea," she exclaimed.

Warbucks shot her a look of annoyance. "It isn't a 'swell idea,' Annie, it's impractical foolishness. Good-hearted and empty-headed. Which parks? Which children? How much will it cost? Who's going to organize it? Who's going to run it?"

"I was hoping you would," said Franklin Roosevelt quietly.

Warbucks was shocked into silence. Was this a joke? He looked from Franklin to Eleanor then back to Franklin again. No, the two of them were perfectly serious.

"Me?" Warbucks pointed an incredulous finger at himself.

"And Annie," said FDR with a sly smile, applying the leverage with a vengeance.

"Leapin' lizards!" cried Annie, hardly daring to breathe.

"Out of the question!" snapped Warbucks.

"How could I help?" demanded Annie, thrilled beyond measure.

"Now wait a minute——" began Warbucks, his face turning purple, but FDR, who knew which side his political biscuit was buttered on, had turned his full attention to Annie.

"You could help us recruit the young people," the president told the eagerly nodding child.

"Now hold everything!" Warbucks was on the edge of exploding. He could see how FDR was using Annie, casting a spell over her with his rhetoric and his voice, but he was powerless to stop him. The president's enthusiasm was as catching as a brush fire, and Annie was burning already.

"Many of them have given up hope, Annie," said the president. "They think their government doesn't care if they live or die. You can help us convince them that, with a little effort on their part—"

"I want to say something!" Warbucks shouted, but in vain. It was too late. Annie was recruited as one of the first members of the Civilian Conservation Corps, which would come to be known as the CCC, the president's favorite work-relief program, in which jobless young men between the ages of eighteen and thirty-five were set to renewing the land, restoring forests, digging ditches, building small dams, sleeping out under the stars, eating decent food, and earning thirty dollars a month.

"You'll help us, too, won't you, Oliver?" implored the president.

"Think of the children. Think of Annie!" put in Mrs. Roosevelt, taking Annie's hand and reaching for Warbucks'.

How could he refuse to take the hand of the First Lady when it was offered to him? But, as her soft fingers closed around his hand and pressed it, as he saw Annie's shining face, filled with ideals of a glorious future under the New Deal, Oliver Warbucks shut his eyes. All he could think of was, how the devil am I going to explain this at the next board meeting of the Republican Club?

Miss Hannigan was feeling a whole lot better, pretty good, in fact. After her tantrum, after locking up the orphans for a day and a half, she woke up smiling again. Because Miss Hannigan remembered something, something important. She had forgotten that she was in possession of a piece of information very much relevant to the case of the orphan girl Annie, as the newspapers were calling her. Very relevant. Crucial, in fact. And she, Miss Hannigan herself, was in *exclusive* possession of said information. She had nearly blurted it out the night she heard Warbucks on the radio, blurted it out to the orphans in her anger.

But that would have been a big mistake. That would have been giving away something valuable for nothing. And this was one valuable nugget, believe you me.

And the beautiful part was this: although the information was hot, there was no need to hurry. It would stay hot. It wasn't going to get cold for a long time, not until Miss Hannigan had figured out a way to make it pay off, and pay off big. She was actually sitting on a gold mine; all she had to do was work out the details and then present the entire thing to Warbucks. He would pay, oh, how he would pay for the evidence and the information Miss Hannigan had been sitting on all these years. She'd been saving it as a present for Annie, for some wonderful day when Annie had been so rotten that she deserved it. A secret weapon, so to speak. Thank heavens she'd never had to use it. Thank heavens she'd been patient. Not patient, smart. Because this was her meal ticket, her entry visa into paradise. Miami, here I come! No more Hudson Street winters for you, old girl. No more whining orphans, lying through their teeth: "We love you, Miss Hannigan." No, it would be afternoons on the beach and nights at the casino and tangos without a break, and shenanigans for Hannigan under a big beach umbrella.

So it was with a light heart that she opened the front door of the Hudson Street Home for Girls, Established 1891. But the couple standing on the doorstep brought the frown right back to her face.

They were so *drab*, this middle-aged man and woman; they looked as though they were going to be a real pain in the duff. The man wore glasses, a nondescript fedora as shapeless as his wife, and a raincoat two sizes too large. The dumpy lady with him could only be wifey; no man ran around with a girlfriend who looked like that. Strictly from Nerdsville, the pair of them.

"Excuse me," said the man in a whiny voice. "Are you the lady who runs this establishment?"

"Unfortunately," snapped Miss Hannigan, immediately on her guard.

"Ten years ago," croaked the woman timidly, "we left our little baby girl on the front step—"

"We were starving," the man cut in. "There was a job, managing a hotel in Maine, but only if we had no children—"

"Wrap it up," snarled Miss Hannigan. "I'm listening to Helen Trent." This was the soap opera that proved what so many women longed to prove, that love *can* live in life at thirty-five . . . and even beyond. And, since Miss Hannigan was well "beyond," she needed all the proof she could get.

"We never meant to leave our little Annie," said the woman, tears forming in her drab eyes.

"Annie?" Miss Hannigan's breath began to shorten.

"Now we have a hardware store in New Jersey, and we could take care of her," the man said.

"We've always loved her," the wife put in.

"You're Annie's *parents?*" Miss Hannigan's eyes were popping out of her head, and she was feeling faint. She had a mental picture of her meal ticket with wings on, flying away to Miami without her.

"Our place isn't fancy," said the woman, twisting an old handkerchief in her nervous fingers, "but it's home. We live over the store."

"There's a yard out back," chimed in the husband.

"We have some chickens," said the wife.

"And a *rooster,*" cried the man with a laugh, pulling off his glasses and his wig and giving a loud crow. Rooster Hannigan, her shiftless brother. And hiding under a similar wig and a shapeless coat was the shapely body of Miss Lily St. Regis, named for the hotel.

Miss Hannigan stared dumbfounded at the giggling pair. "Rooster! I never would have recognized you!"

And, in her mind's eye, she saw the meal ticket flying back from Miami, and it had a nice suntan.

CHAPTER ELEVEN

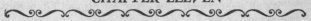

But before Miss Hannigan could figure out a way to use Rooster and Lily in her plans, or even make plans, *they* put the moves on *her*. It turned out that crafty Rooster and curvy Lily had decided to go for the big scam, Warbucks' reward money. That's what the corny getup was all about.

"If we can fool you, sis, we can fool Bigbucks," Rooster told her earnestly, leaning over the desk.

"Fifty thousand smackers," and Lily licked her catlike chops at the mere mention of the words.

Miss Hannigan heard them out and sipped at her gin, saying nothing. But her brain was chugging a mile a minute up the grade. This put a whole new light on things. There were definite possibilities here. Hannigan had only been thinking vaguely of peddling her secret information to Warbucks, but what Rooster had in mind was far more audacious and a lot nastier. She was beginning to like it, but she still sat silent and shook her head. No point in looking too eager. Besides, she had no use for Miss Walbarf-Castoria in the low-cut polkadot blouse, sitting there, draped over Rooster like he was furniture.

"Aw, sis," Rooster turned on his never-fail charm, "this is gonna be the best bunco job ever. All we need is details."

"About Annie. Specifics," the floozy chimed in.

Miss Hannigan leaned back in her chair and eyeballed the pair of them. "What's in it for me?" she asked.

Rooster's grin split his ratty little face right in half. Now she was talking!

"Money. A three-way split of the fifty thou."

Miss Hannigan shook her head uh-uh. "I want half."

"Half!?!" squeaked Lily, all fluffy indignation.

117

But Rooster knew a bargain when he saw it. "All right, half," he conceded briskly. Besides, promising to pay and actually paying off are two very different things.

"Rooster!" protested Lily, but Rooster waved a shushing hand in her direction.

"It's all right. Twenty-five grand for me and Lil, twenty-five grand for you."

"Let's see what she has first. See if it's worth twenty-five grand," pouted Lily.

Miss Hannigan threw her a look of contempt. With what she herself knew that nobody else did, and Rooster's way with a con game, the money seemed in the bag. Why not? Let Rooster and Lily do the dirty work, lay themselves on the line. Miss Hannigan would sit back quietly and collect. But she resented every penny that would go to Rooster's cuddly little fuzzball, and she longed to drop a cyanide capsule in Lily's Moxie.

"I got specifics on every kid in this dump." She stood up and made her way into the small, crowded storeroom attached to her office. The walls of the storeroom were floor-to-ceiling shelves, and the shelves were crowded with piled-up and dusty boxes, boxes which had sat there unopened for years.

"It's just a question of finding the right box," she said, waving at the shelves. "Now listen to me, and listen good, because what I got is worth a lot more than fifty thousand dollars. Annie's parents are dead, see? Nobody knows that except me. They were killed in a fire, years and years ago. The cops brought me all their junk, and it's in there somewhere. Two boxes full, as I recall.

"I read all the newspaper stories and listened to all the radio reports. There's two things that Warbucks and Annie left out of the story. Which orphanage she came from and why she wears that old broken locket around her neck. Her parents had saved the other half to claim her with. I figure they left those things out on purpose, to make sure the real parents turned up. Well, the real parents aren't *ever* turning up, but only we know that. And, my darling Rooster, if Annie's so-called parents can claim her with that locket, so can we!" She flashed her brother an evil grin of triumph.

Lily drew her breath in. It was beautiful, foolproof!

They were the only ones with the key to all that money; the legit claimants were playing harp duets somewhere above the clouds. Oh, that was worth half the money any day.

"Fifty thousand smackers," she breathed out, her voice caressing the money as though it were in bed with her.

"And the kid we'll drop in the river," chortled Rooster.

"It can't miss," agreed his sister.

Now the only thing Miss Hannigan hadn't taken into her calculations were those miserable orphans. She should have known better. She knew they had ways of learning everything; their wretched little eyes and ears were everywhere. They had cut peepholes and earholes all over the ancient building; why did she keep forgetting that? Also, the building was heated (when it *was* heated, which was never in the winter) by forced hot air, and there were ducts and vents in almost every room, which carried voices clearly. But Miss Hannigan never took that into consideration. She should have known better, but she hated those orphans so, that she pushed them out of her mind whenever she could.

Molly, scrubbing out the upstairs bathroom, heard voices coming out of the vent—Miss Hannigan's and two strangers'—but, being only six years old, she didn't pay much attention to them until she heard Annie's name mentioned. Then she listened as hard as she could, in growing alarm, until Rooster declared he planned to throw Annie in the river. Molly dropped her brush and gave a shrill little squeal of fear.

"Pepper!" she yelled, because Pepper was on bathroom detail with her, "they're gonna do something bad to Annie!"

Pepper gave an elaborate yawn. Annie had never been her favorite, and she was sick to death of hearing about her. Annie This and Annie That and Annie was going to live like a millionaire, and now Annie had stubbed her toe or something stupid like that. "Did you clean out the can?" she ordered.

Molly sniffled, but there was no way that a six-year-old could take on a thirteen-year-old, so she picked up her scrub brush and the pail and got back to work.

Downstairs, the Unholy Three were tearing the supply

closet apart, ripping up the boxes and dumping their con
tents out on the floor. Litter was everywhere, but so far
no luck. "It was in an envelope, a sealed envelope," Mis
Hannigan was saying nervously. She grabbed another stac
of boxes off the shelves. "Look in those," she ordered Lily
shoving them at her. "Make yourself useful. It'll have he
name on it."

Lily took the boxes and began to look slowly throug
them. Rooster and Miss Hannigan dug through their stack
frantically, looking for the envelope only, but Lily too
her time, examining everything in every box, and tuckin
away in her dress any little pathetic heirloom that caugh
her rapacious eye. In the fourth box she opened, she cam
upon a white envelope, creased and bulging. On it wa
scribbled in pencil a single word: Annie. Teasingly, sh
held it up in the air and waited for the other two t
notice it. When they did, Rooster gave a loud crow
grabbed it away from her, and ripped it open.

There was nothing in it but half a locket.

For a long, awed minute, they crowded around it, look
ing at their ticket of admission, the cheap little broke
trinket that spelled Easy Street.

"We got it," said Lily triumphantly.

"We got it!" yelled Rooster and Lily.

"WE GOT IT!!" the three of them shrieked, then Roost
er broke again into his evil cock-crow, a sure sign tha
something wicked was going to happen.

Upstairs, her ear to the bathroom vent, Molly felt th
hair on the back of her neck prickle. Pepper or no Peppe
she had to get out of here and warn Annie. She stood u
as quietly as she could, and laid her brush down. Sh
peeked around the corner of the toilet cubicle to see Pep
per sitting on the floor, smoking a homemade cigarette an
goofing off. Pepper's back was turned. Molly picked u
Pepper's mop and swung it with all her little might, clip
ping Pepper on the ear and putting her temporarily out o
business. Then she fled past her into the dormitory, wher
the rest of them were stealing a break, now that Hanniga
was locked up on business downstairs.

"They're gonna do something bad to Annie!" yelle
Molly, bursting in. The other girls looked up, startled.

"Who is?" demanded Duffy.

"*They* are!" yelled Molly, pointing at the bathroom. She meant, of course, the people who owned the voices coming out of the hot-air register, but she was too little to get that out right away.

"Who's they?" Kate asked again.

Molly was wriggling all over with frustration. She knew they were wasting time. "Come *on*, you guys," she urged. "We gotta warn her! We gotta hurry!"

One by one the orphans got to their feet. If Molly's words hadn't convinced them, Molly's face and the anxiety in her voice had. It was clear: They had to warn Annie. Of what, they'd find out later. But now that Miss Hannigan was out of the way for a while, it was a good opportunity to hit the trail. They made for the window, which gave onto an old-fashioned iron fire escape. One by one—even Pepper—they climbed on the wrought-iron landing and began to go down the stairs. Orphans to the rescue.

Down in Miss Hannigan's quarters, the conspirators were celebrating. Having tanked themselves up on the new brew, they'd put on the radio and danced, Miss St. Regis throwing a mean cancan, and Miss Hannigan hopping around on her stork legs imagining she was Isadora Duncan. Easy Street was their new address, and they were planning to move there that very afternoon, right after they picked up Annie and the money, disposing of one and dividing the other.

As Miss Hannigan danced, movement caught the corner of her eye. Movement outside her window. "Hey," she said shakily, and staggered over to see. What she saw sobered her. A bunch of those miserable orphans was tiptoeing down the fire escape, right past her very nose, making their escape. Of all the nerve! Sounding her battle cry: "Kill! kill! kill!" she dashed out the door.

As they rounded the corner, the girls could hear Miss Hannigan pounding after them, shrieking. They ran faster, all except Molly, whose stubby little baby legs wouldn't carry her any faster. Molly was falling behind and getting out of breath in the bargain. Suddeny, a bony hand like a falcon's talons clutched the child's shoulder. Miss Hannigan! Caught!

"I got Molly," Miss Hannigan called out tauntingly to the others. Reluctantly, they stopped running, stood there, half a block ahead of her, uncertain of what to do. Annie or Molly? Molly or Annie?

"No!" yelled Molly at the top of her lungs. "Go on! I'm okay! Go *on!*" She struggled in Miss Hannigan's strong arms, trying to find an opening to kick the woman's shins, or even to step on her toe. But Hannigan promptly clapped a hand over the child's mouth, and held her wriggling body at arm's length, tantalizingly, so that the orphans could see it. And it worked.

One by one, the girls straggled back, defeated. Miss Hannigan collected them with a triumphant cackle and marched them back inside. Then she dragged them up to the top floor and locked them into a tiny, airless closet, which was littered with boxes and mouse droppings, and threw away the key.

"All right," said Pepper into the darkness. "Whose rotten idea was this?"

987 Fifth Avenue was a shambles; it bore little resemblance to the stately mansion it had been this morning. Rather, it looked like a village after a horde of insane elephants had thundered through it on a rampage. Precious Ming vases lay in shards. Pictures hung askew; the walls were covered with grimy fingermarks and the lustrous marble floors were covered by a scuffed mantle of footprints. Cigarette butts were everywhere—on the mantels, in the potted palms, stubbed out in priceless bibelots.

Grace Farrell sighed and put down her pencil. In front of her on the card table was a mountain of questionnaires, hours' worth of paperwork and discouragement. Around her, she could see the servants tackling the mess with mops and pails, vacuum cleaners and polishes. They were as angry and depressed as she was. It would take hours to make a dent in this mess, and days before the extent of the damage could be assessed. And most of the damaged things were priceless, therefore uninsurable, therefore uninsured.

Yet these were, in the last analysis, only *things*. But how to face Annie? How to tell Annie that among all the hundreds and hundreds of people who came clamoring for the money none of them had emerged as her true parents? Miss Farrell sighed again.

Outside and above the house, the noise of the autocopter was at first faint, barely discernible, like the buzzing of a faraway hive of bees. But it grew closer and louder; they were coming back from Washington.

Oh, dear, thought Miss Farrell. If only they'd stayed longer! Given the servants a few more hours to get this mess straightened out. Mr. Warbucks . . . Oliver . . . would be furious!

And it was true. When Warbucks walked into the room with Annie and the Asp, Punjab following, the look of astonishment on his face turned to a deep scowl of displeasure. But Annie didn't notice a thing. Her face was lit up by excitement, and she was chattering to Punjab.

"Maybe they brought me a sister and a brother. Maybe they—"

Punjab put a gentle hand on Annie's curly head. "Buddha says that man who counts his chickens before they're hatched is a scrambled egg," he told her gently. But Annie wasn't paying attention. Spotting Grace, she ran over to her at once, eyes questioning.

"Is my mother pretty? Is my father tall? What are they like? What do they do? Are they the grandest people you ever met?" she demanded all in one breath.

Miss Farrell bit her lips and exchanged glances with Mr. Warbucks. Drake, noticing this, signaled silently to the other servants. "We'll finish later." And the maids and footmen filed out swiftly.

Grace, looking with sympathy at the excited child, decided that the most direct way was the kindest. "We haven't found them, Annie."

Annie paled, and the excitement drained out of her face, leaving it without color or life. She seemed to grow shorter and younger, and a weak little smile trembled on her lips before it disappeared entirely.

Grace's heart ached for her, and she turned to Oliver Warbucks with tears in her eyes.

"I've interviewed eight hundred and sixty-five couples," she said, indicating the card table piled high with papers. "None of them knew about the locket. I never realized how many dishonest people there were in New York." Discouragement was written all over her pretty features.

Warbucks sighed, and his hand touched Annie's hair briefly and gently. He, too, felt deeply for the child's pain, but he was more experienced and more cynical than Grace, and his disappointment wasn't aggravated by disillusion, as was hers.

Annie suddenly needed to be alone, very alone. She ducked out from under Oliver Warbucks' hand and made a bolt for the stairs, Sandy bounding along after her. Grace uttered a small cry and started after her, but Warbucks laid a restraining hand on her arm.

"I'll go," he said quietly, and he mounted the stairs to Annie's bedroom.

The child was sitting forlornly on the windowseat of her room, her dog in her arms. She had evidently been fighting a losing battle with her tears, for Sandy was busily licking the salt from his little mistress's face.

The look on Annie's face caught Mr. Warbucks in the solar plexus, like a blow. Until this moment, he'd not realized how important her optimism, her enthusiasm for everything, was to him. She represented his lost youth, his vanished ideals. Making her happy was like making some long-hidden part of himself happy, too. And seeing her so unhappy was like having that hidden part of him die a little. And he felt so damn helpless, that was the worst part of it! He loved her, and he could do nothing for her.

"Annie," he said gently from the doorway.

She didn't look up at him, but stared straight ahead of her. "I guess they're dead," she said without emphasis, her voice lifeless. "I guess I've known that deep down for a long time."

"I'm not giving up!" Warbucks told her stoutly. "Don't you give up."

But Annie shook her head sadly. "I didn't want to be just another orphan, Mr. Warbucks," she told him. "I wanted to believe I was special—"

Crossing the room in two swift bounds, Warbucks caught hold of Annie's shoulders and turned her to face him.

"You *are* special," he said fiercely. "Don't ever stop believing that! You are special to me, special to all of us and special to yourself. It's the most important weapon you have in the fight! Do you believe that? Annie, look at me! Do you believe that?" His eyes probed deeply into hers, forcing her to meet his gaze.

Without a word, Annie burst into tears and threw her arms around Oliver Warbucks' neck, clinging to him and crying bitterly. Sandy set up a furor of barking and licking, trying to get at Annie's face to comfort it.

Warbucks sat holding the little girl he had come to love so much, rocking her in his arms, patting and stroking her shoulders, and feeling very, very much like "Daddy." After a while, the great sobs became tears and the tears sniffles, and at last the crying ended. Annie sat up and dried her eyes on Mr. Warbucks' clean linen handkerchief, and blew her nose, and smiled a little, and patted Sandy, and felt a whole lot better. Crying does that sometimes, especially if you're not much of a crier.

"Well!" said Warbucks brightly, standing up. "Shall we go downstairs?"

Annie nodded.

Downstairs, there was a ring at the doorbell. Punjab opened the front door and looked down from his enormous height onto a small, rather dim-looking couple. The woman was clutching the man's arm fearfully, and the man himself bore a striking resemblance to Casper Milquetoast, the Timid Soul of the funny papers. Yet, small and unprepossessing as the couple was, Punjab felt a warning prickle under his turban.

"Is this the Warbucks home?" asked the man.

"It is," said Punjab distantly.

"We've come for our little girl," said the woman. "We've come for Annie."

"This way, please," and he led them into the living room, where Grace looked up annoyed. Another pair of deceivers, for she couldn't imagine them to be anything else. A couple of deadbeats who came out of the woodwork to exploit a poor little orphan child for gain. Her thoughts surprised her, but Grace Farrell had had a rough morning, and it was late in the day and she was weary. If nothing else, today had been a bitter educational experience.

They started on their tale of woe immediately, and it was the same one she'd heard over and over today, a young couple down on their luck, unable to care for their one and only child. This one had a variation too boring to talk about, a job in Maine somewhere, but no children allowed. She wasn't buying word one of the tale.

"We were starving, ma'am," Rooster whined pathetically. "We needed the job, even though it meant—"

Grace had heard all she cared to. "Punjab," she called, so that the giant could escort the pair to the front door.

"—leaving our baby girl," continued Rooster.

"—wrapped in a newspaper—" contributed Lily.

"—on the steps of the Hudson Street orphanage," Rooster finished all in one breath.

An immediate and heavy silence fell, in which Punjab and Grace exchanged glances of consternation. Could it be possible? There was something so obviously fishy about this couple, and yet they had said the magic words; they knew the name of Annie's orphanage. What to do next?

Annie and Warbucks were coming down the marble stairway, followed by Sandy.

"What's this?" asked Warbucks as he came into the living room, scowling.

Grace consulted her notes. "Ralph and Shirley Mudge, Mr. Warbucks. From Hoboken, New Jersey."

Sandy growled. His instincts were all telling him that something here was smelling funny. Mr. Warbucks didn't care for the look of them either, but he shook the limp hand that "Ralph Mudge" was holding out to him.

There was a soft commotion, as "Shirley Mudge" caught sight of Annie and began to flutter around her husband.

"Oh, Ralph," she pointed breathlessly. "Do you think that's our Annie? Our very own little girl?"

Purposefully, Miss Farrell picked up a handful of paper.

"If you'll just fill out this questionnaire—" she began, but the Mudges weren't paying attention.

"Oh, Ralph, look!" cried Lily sweetly. "She still has the locket!" While Grace and Oliver stood by in shock, Lily St. Regis trotted over to Annie, dug in her purse, and came out with the other half. She held it up to the locket around Annie's neck, and the two halves fitted perfectly together. Then she smiled breathlessly into Annie's face.

"We've finally found you!"

Annie gave a sharp cry. But instead of throwing herself into her mother's arms, as she'd dreamed of doing for so many years, she turned and buried her face in Oliver Warbucks' waistcoat.

CHAPTER TWELVE

What else was there to do? Ralph and Shirley Mudge might not have looked like much, but they certainly satisfied the requirements. Not only did they know where Annie had been abandoned, but they had produced the missing half of the locket. Ergo, they must be Annie's parents, Q.E.D.

Annie Mudge. She tried it out in her mind, but it had a funny sound and an even funnier feeling. This was all so different from what Annie had imagined. In her mind, her mother had always been beautiful and sweet-looking, like Grace Farrell, and lately her mental image of her father had worn a commanding air and a bald head.

But she didn't mean to be ungrateful. These were her real parents, and they couldn't help how they looked. Annie had never been one to place good looks above everything that counted; if she had, she never would have picked up Sandy. But it was more than only their looks, or the fact that their manners were crude. Annie knew she must come from very poor folks; why else would they have left their baby at an orphanage? Poverty was no crime, and neither was lack of education or culture. *I'm spoiled; that's what's wrong with me,* thought Annie. *Spoiled and ungrateful. It's just that I've waited for this day to come for so long, and now that it's here . . . it's so . . . different from what I'd imagined.*

And yet . . . and yet . . . there was something else, something she couldn't put her finger on. But Sandy was still growling, and Punjab had that look on his face, and Grace looked so unhappy, and Mr. Warbucks was scowling like a thundercloud.

Oliver Warbucks had done a lot of business with a lot of shady types and had developed an instinct for spotting them that didn't take a back seat to Sandy's. He knew these two were shady, but unfortunately they were Annie's parents and his hands were tied. It wasn't that he thought they were lying about who they were; didn't they have the only proof? No, what Warbucks believed was that they had come to claim their little girl only because of the fifty thousand reward. If there had been no money, they would have left Annie to rot in the orphanage.

And these were the people he was supposed to entrust his precious little Annie to! The thought cut him like a knife, and evidently others were of the same opinion, because Grace was positively suffering, and Punjab looked unhappy, and Sandy was down on his belly with his neck hairs raised, and only the Asp was inscrutable, as usual.

Still, he had no choice. Alarmed as Warbucks was for Annie's safety and well-being, what legal recourse had he against the child's natural parents?

"I suppose you heard about the reward on the radio?" he asked Mr. Mudge.

Rooster forced his face to look surprised. "There's a reward?"

"We don't have a radio," "Shirley" put in meekly.

"You saw the newspapers, then."

"Papers? What papers?" asked Rooster innocently.

"How did you know that Annie was here?" asked Grace.

"Some dame at the orphanage told us," said Rooster.

Lily dug around in her shabby pocketbook, coming up with a worn and folded piece of paper, which she handed to Warbucks.

"Here's her birth certificate. I've kept it next to my heart all these years," she said. Actually, she'd found it in the same shoebox with the locket only a few hours before.

Unfolding it carefully, Oliver read aloud, " 'Ann Marie Mudge. Born October 18, 1922.' "

Now Annie spoke up for the first time. "I'll go pack," she said quietly, and started out of the room.

"Want me to help, baby?" cooed Lily.

Annie stopped. "No, thanks. Mom," she added. The word sounded strange on her tongue. Slowly, she headed for the stairs.

Oliver Warbucks led the way into his library, where he opened the top drawer of a massive desk and took out a scrap of paper, holding it so that Ralph Mudge and his wife could see it clearly.

"A certified check?" Rooster's eyebrows lifted. "Sir, we're just so thrilled to have found Annie, we don't need any money," he simpered piously.

Bushwah, thought Warbucks, but all he said was, "Then I'll take it back."

Before the words were out of his mouth, Lily's soft little hand had snaked out and fastened over the check.

"Of course, we are poor people. It would help us a lot. We could buy Annie milk and a warm blanket—"

Spare me, thought Warbucks. *Don't insult my intelligence.* Out loud he said, "Put it in your pocket, Mrs. Mudge."

The check vanished like a snowflake on a sizzling stove top, and there was nothing left to say. In silence, they waited for Annie to come down, Warbucks and Grace lost in gloomy thoughts, Rooster and Lily trying to keep their glee from showing on their faces. The scam had gone off without a hitch! Easy Street, here we come!

The orphanage had been quiet for hours. It must be very late, but to the unhappy girls sandwiched into the uncomfortable supply closet, the hours had dragged by like years. They had no idea what time it was, or even if it was the very same day. Molly had told them everything she'd learned from the bathroom vent, and they'd pieced the rest of the story together, and it was obvious that Annie was in very bad trouble indeed. Molly was right. They *had* to warn her. But what if it was already too late? They couldn't think about that. They had to get out.

But how? Miss Hannigan had locked them in tightly, and that door was the only way in or out. It looked hopeless.

Suddenly, Pepper cried, "Look!" and pointed up. They followed her finger. There was a kind of trapdoor on the ceiling of the closet, and it probably led to the roof. But how to reach it? The closet was narrow but high; these old buildings had tall rooms, and there was no ladder.

Unless . . . they agreed. The largest and strongest on the bottom, the smallest on top. That meant that Pepper took the firmest stance she could and braced herself. July, the next largest, climbed up onto Pepper's shoulders and wavered there. Kate climbed up over Pepper and July, and stationed herself. Duffy, who was small but wiry, scrambled up over the human ladder and tried to open the trapdoor. It hadn't been opened in years, and it wouldn't budge. It was dark and stuffy at the top of the closet, and what little air there was was choked with cobwebs and dust, and that didn't help Duffy's struggles any. Under her, the girls were beginning to groan and wobble and call advice up to her.

"Put your back into it!" yelled Pepper.

"Hurry up!" pleaded Kate. "I can't take much more of this."

"I'm doing the best I can," Duffy shouted down. "This is no picnic, y'know."

The dust was getting to her, filling her nose and eyes with terrible itchings. Duffy opened her mouth to sneeze, shut it again, opened it, and out issued a sneeze like the roar of a lion. The human ladder wobbled and almost fell, but Duffy shot upward on the force of the sneeze. Her hard little head struck the edge of the trapdoor in just exactly the right spot, and the hatch flew open!

Duffy scrambled through it and found herself on the roof, just as they'd hoped.

"It's all right," she called back down. "C'mon up."

Molly was sent up first, as the smallest, then Tessie, who was murmuring, "Oh, my goodness, oh, my goodness," as usual. Kate climbed through the opening, then they reached down and pulled July through.

That left only Pepper, and she had an uncomfortable climb up a hot-water pipe before she, too, popped like a cork out of the trapdoor and onto the roof. Now they were there, but where were they? They ran to the edge of the roof and looked down.

The late-summer sun had set less than an hour ago, and it was that strange hour between the sunset and the moonrise that is called twilight and has a special radiance all its own. There was still some light to see by, but it was fast fading. Below them, three stories down, they could see the street, and the alleyways, and a handful of people who'd had their supper (the orphans, of course, hadn't) and were out again in the warm evening.

In order to get off the roof, they'd have to climb down

the drainpipe; there was no other way. It was perilous and terrifying, but these were no ordinary girls. These were orphans who'd never known decent treatment; they had developed a certain amount of toughness, independence, and courage. They were scared, sure, but what choice did they have? One after the other, they set out on the long road down, sliding down the rough iron drainpipe, grabbing at a clothesline to swing over, dropping to the next roof, from that roof down to a metal awning and from the awning, down to the street. Pepper led the way; Annie might not have been her favorite person, but now that she was in danger, it was up to the orphans to take care of their own. The girls took turns handing Molly down until, as though by a miracle, they all stood safe and sound on the sidewalk.

Now all they had to do was find Annie.

The radio had given the address of Oliver Warbucks' mansion, and they knew in a vague way that it was uptown on the east side and they were downtown on the west. Without carfare for the trolley, all they could do was walk. As it was going to be a long, long walk, they'd better not waste time. And so they set out, six ragged little girls with one sense of purpose and, they hoped, a decent sense of direction.

"I'll go see what's keeping Annie," volunteered Grace, glad to leave the unspoken tension of the situation. Upstairs, she found Annie putting the last of her things into her suitcase and trying to put a brave face on things.

"We're still going to be friends, aren't we, Miss Farrell?"

"Of course, Annie, we'll always be friends."

"And now that I'll have a home of my own, I can have you come to visit, you and Mr. Warbucks. Will you come?"

"We'd love to." Grace tried hard to smile; she owed Annie that, at least. Not to break down in front of her.

"It's gonna be all right, you'll see. They're real nice folks, I can tell. I'm gonna love living in New Jersey."

"Of course you are, darling. Who wouldn't love living in New Jersey?"

✦   ✦   ✦

They'd been walking for what seemed like hours, and it was starting to rain, one of those swift, ferocious, merciless summer rains that come pelting at you from a suddenly angry sky, driven by gusting winds and punctuated by green and blue lightning. There was a park ahead of them and an arch, and they huddled under it unhappily, waiting for the rain to stop. They waited a very long time before it was safe to come out, but finally creeping from their insufficient shelter they made their way across the street and onto a broad boulevard that seemed to begin right there.

"Oh, my goodness," said Tessie for the seven hundredth time.

"We're never gonna make it," predicted Pepper dourly.

But Duffy had spotted a street sign and was trying to read it with some difficulty. It was dark, the sign was wet with rain, and she couldn't read all that well, anyway. But at last it clicked into place, the letters held a meaning.

"We've found Fifth Avenue!" she turned to the others and exulted.

Pepper looked at the house number on the nearest building's canopy. "Number One, Fifth Avenue," she read. "We gotta get to *Nine Hundred and Eighty-seven!*"

They groaned and plodded on.

The moment was here, and it couldn't be put off any longer. Annie's bag was packed, she was dressed to go, and go they must. When they walked out the front door and Annie saw the battered 1929 Ford pickup truck sitting between the proud Town Car and the haughty Dusenberg, she felt a pang of disappointment, followed by anger at herself for her snobbery. Didn't she know there was a depression on?

Mr. and Mrs. Mudge bundled Sandy into the open part of the truck, and Rooster slid behind the wheel. Lily gestured for Annie to slide in after her, then she climbed into the cab next to Rooster and snuggled close. Annie felt mighty left out of things, and desperately sad as she took last looks at Grace, Punjab, and the Asp. Mr. Warbucks was nowhere to be seen; he had made his good-byes inside, and wished to be alone with his grief. But he was watching, from the balcony outside his office, as the old pickup began to drive away, and there was a suspicious wetness in his eyes.

But they didn't go far, only around the corner, where Rooster stepped on the brake and the pickup came to a stop. An old lady with a shopping bag came hobbling out of the shadows and climbed onto the running board with surprising agility. She yanked the truck door open and slid in next to Annie, who was now squeezed between her and Lily, and getting more and more bewildered, especially as her "mother" and "father" began to peel pieces of their disguise off. "Mom" snatched off her dowdy hat and wig, revealing a head of blonde hair, while "Dad" threw off his eyeglasses and his beady little eyes glittered.

"Did you get it, Rooster?" screeched the bag lady, in a voice so unmistakable that Annie's blood froze in her veins. Miss Hannigan! No two ways about it, that's gotta be Miss Hannigan's voice!

The woman who had posed as Annie's mother was waving the certified check under the bag lady's nose. Miss Hannigan snatched it.

"*I'll* hold it. For safe keeping."

The younger woman, quick as a hungry cat on a plump mouse, snatched it back.

"Over my dead body."

"Over anything," snarled Miss Hannigan, grabbing the check again.

Sensing that this might be her only chance, Annie made a leap across Miss Hannigan and grabbed the handle of the truck door, but the woman was too fast and too strong, and grabbed her tight.

"Help! Mr. Warbucks! Help me!" yelled Annie, shouting as loud as she could. Miss Hannigan's hand clamped over her mouth.

Rooster jammed the truck into gear and they took off into the night, swift as a bat.

Oh, thought Annie. *Oh, no, no. Where are they taking me? What are they going to do with me?*

They had come about three miles, two of them up Fifth Avenue, and they were exhausted. Hungry, cold, stiff, and totally worn out, their feet aching, bodies begging for sleep. Yet they were only as far uptown as Forty-second Street, and they still had nearly two more miles to go. When they reached the broad steps of the New York Public Library's main building, the orphans simply collapsed, sprawling on the marble stairs, unable to go on. Maybe this expedition had been crazy in the first place; they were too tired to trust their judgment. It seemed to them that they would never reach Oliver Warbucks' house, never be able to warn Annie in time. It was probably too late by now anyway.

Annie watched horrified as Lily and Rooster and Miss Hannigan discarded what was left of their disguises. Two of the three she had never seen before, but if they were only half as bad as Miss Hannigan, Annie's goose was cooked. They sat jammed together in the front seat, and Annie was scared and uncomfortable, and unable to think. Sandy was in the back . . . she hoped . . . but she hadn't seen him or heard him in a long while. Anything might have happened. She felt very small and very alone.

Merriment was rising all around her, as the conspirators began to realize that they'd really pulled it off, really gotten away with the fifty thousand bucks. Now all they had to do was figure out how to spend it.

"I wanna get me one of them little gold lamé numbers," said the cheap little blonde who had called herself Shirley Mudge.

"If they sell them in Atlantic City. We're not stopping until we get to Atlantic City," laughed the skinny little ferret of a man Miss Hannigan had called Rooster.

Atlantic City! What am I gonna do in Atlantic City? moaned Annie silently. She wasn't even sure where Atlantic City was. She wasn't even sure where they were right this minute.

Where they were was Fifth Avenue at Forty-second Street, heading downtown past the library. As a matter of fact, they were driving right on by the orphans at this moment, but they couldn't see Annie because she was jammed between the others on the front seat, and she couldn't see them for the same reason. But Sandy saw them, and he began to whine.

* * *

135

"I say we go back," said Pepper gloomily.

"We *can't*," came from Molly.

"We been walking for a hundred years," Kate sighed.

"Yeah, and we're never gonna get there," Pepper stated vehemently, bringing the others way down.

"We *have* to!" Molly was still keeping the faith.

"Let's take a vote," suggested Duffy.

"All those in favor of calling it quits," said Pepper, raising her own hand. Kate voted with her, then nervous little Tessie, and finally a reluctant July raised her grubby hand. Four to two, with Duffy and Molly outvoted. They'd go back. It was probably too late to do anything for Annie anyway. They never saw the pickup truck passing by, or the whining dog inside the back.

As the distance grew between him and the orphans, Sandy made up his mind. He wanted with all his doggy heart to stay with Annie, especially since he knew she was surrounded by danger. Those were bad people with her; he could sense it. Miss Hannigan he knew of old, but as soon as he'd laid eyes on Rooster and Lily, back there in Mr. Warbucks' home, he'd known they were not good guys. Annie needed him now more than ever.

But when he saw the orphans outside the library, sprawled on the steps, he sensed that Annie's only salvation lay in bringing help. It was the conflict inside him that caused him to scratch and whine, and it was the resolution of that conflict that caused him to leap out of the pickup truck and run the four blocks back to the library.

"It's Sandy! Look, everybody, it's Sandy."

And he was jumping up and licking faces and barking loudly.

"He wants something," said Duffy.

Sandy would run a few steps off, then turn and bark furiously, then run back, then run off again barking.

"He wants us to follow him!" Molly cried.

"Then what are we waiting for? Let's go!" yelled Pepper, who a moment ago had been all for returning to the orphanage. But that was forgotten now, as they followed Sandy at a run. He raced up Fifth Avenue, north, as the truck holding Annie prisoner headed south.

It was a long run, but the little girls had their second

wind now, and, with Molly on Kate's back, they managed to keep up pretty well with the dog. Whenever he got too far ahead of them, he'd turn and wait, barking at the orphans to please hurry.

Eventually they got there, to Oliver Warbucks' mansion, to the high iron gates and the thick stone wall. But nothing stopped Sandy. Squeezing in between the bars of the gates, he ran around the huge pillars and up to the front portico. The orphans, one by one, did the same. Ahead of them was the massive wooden door, and Sandy, on his hind legs, was scratching and barking at it.

Now that they were finally here, the little girls were terrified. What would Mr. Warbucks say? What would they dare to say to him? They stared at one another in panic, until Pepper, the oldest, hiked up her skirt and marched up to the front door and rang the bell hard.

"Now what?" scowled Oliver Warbucks. He really wanted to be alone tonight; he had no patience with anything or anybody. Annie was gone, and he would have to pick up the pieces of his life tomorrow. As for tonight, just let him alone.

Punjab and the Asp went to the door together, and Punjab pulled it open. There was Sandy, barking furiously, and Punjab knew he'd been right. The little Princess was in trouble somewhere. But where? Behind Sandy, he could see a little group of anxious faces, six raggedy little orphans, staring at him in terror. Nobody had told them there would be a man as big as a mountain and all black. Did he eat little girls? They just stood there trembling, with their mouths hanging open, much as Annie herself had done when she'd first laid eyes on Punjab.

Suddenly, Oliver Warbucks appeared in the doorway at Punjab's side. The man they'd come to see, and now they were too scared to speak to him.

"Sandy!" Warbucks exclaimed. "What are you doing here?"

"Sir . . ." began Molly in a tiny little voice.

Kate jabbed her in the ribs. "I think he's a Highness," she whispered.

"Your Highness," Molly whispered.

"We're friends of Annie's," said Duffy bravely.

Warbucks frowned deeply, and the lines around his

mouth tugged the corners down. "She's gone," he said flatly. "Her parents came and got her. They—"

"That wasn't her parents, mister!" Molly cut in excitedly. "They was bad peoples." She saw Oliver Warbucks' eyes open wide, and then the giant had her by the shoulders and was glaring into her face, willing her to say more. He *did* eat little girls. Molly fainted dead away.

Punjab lifted her gently and carried the tiny girl into the house, with the other orphans trailing behind him and the Asp.

As for Oliver Warbucks, he was running for the stairs, shouting for Grace, shouting for the servants, the police, the army, navy, and marine corps. The entire house was galvanized into action.

Because Rooster was the strongest of them, it was decided that he should keep hold of Annie, and so he and Lily changed places, Lily taking the wheel, while Rooster sat jammed close to Annie, his hands digging roughly into the flesh of the little girl's arms. The truck was way downtown now, where the office buildings yield their places to docks, piers, and warehouses, totally deserted at night, except for rats of the rodent and human kind.

"Rooster, honey," whined Lily, squirming in her seat. "It's so cramped in here, my dress is getting all sweaty. Let's get rid of the kid and make some room."

"Okey-dokey," chortled Rooster.

Lily put on the brake and the truck rumbled to a stop in a totally empty street filled with vacant lots and chain-link fences. Rooster opened the door, and Annie, sensing that her final hour might be at hand, began to fight like a tiger, flailing out with her tiny fists, and kicking and squirming.

"Mr. Warbucks is gonna knock your lights out!" she hollered. "Mr. Warbucks is gonna rearrange your teeth. Mr. Warbucks is gonna cut off your—"

Suddenly, she saw her chance. Miss Hannigan was holding the check as she, too, struggled with Annie, and Annie reached up and snatched it out of her surprised hand, pushed her aside, and leaped down from the truck. She ran, pounding hard, down the old cobbled street that hurt her shoes and twisted her ankles. She dodged around fences and darted through an alley, her breath coming fast and her sides aching. But she was getting away! She was getting away!

Annie ran around a corner and smack into Rooster Hannigan, who was waiting for her with a twisted smile on his ugly face. He grabbed her roughly and bent her arm up her back until she yelled in pain. Then he marched her back to the truck, and his evil chuckle made Annie's blood run cold in her veins. Oh, she was trapped all right!

CHAPTER THIRTEEN

The orphans were quickly and efficiently debriefed by Warbucks and Grace, and now Oliver Warbucks knew everything they knew. The culprits were Miss Hannigan and another pair, the couple posing as Annie's parents. The truck had last been seen heading south on Fifth Avenue, a few blocks down from Forty-second Street. The orphans were wrapped in blankets and taken down to the kitchen for Mrs. Pugh to feed from the huge steaming pots of good things she kept on the stove.

Warbucks swung into action. It was his element, action, and he felt almost happy. At least he was doing something, barking commands into the telephone, using his clout, exercising his power. He felt almost elated, larger than life. Annie—*his* Annie, because she wasn't anybody else's—was in danger, and by God he'd get her out of it if it cost him his last million dollars. Mobilization, that was the ticket. All units operating and in communication.

"You take the autocopter, I'll take the car," Warbucks commanded Punjab as he held the phone for J. Edgar Hoover, head of the Federal Bureau of Investigation. Hoover came on the wire. "Yes, J. Edgar, Warbucks here. The orphan, Annie, has been kidnapped. I want every G-man east of the Mississippi on this case in the next twenty minutes. Yes? Good."

The coast guard was assigned to all ports of exit; the New York mounted police to do a block by block search south of Forty-second Street, while squad cars of New York's Finest set up roadblocks. The train stations and bus terminals were covered. So the criminals couldn't escape. But that was only the mop-up operation under way, to prevent them from getting away with the money. But something could be happening to Annie this very minute,

140

and who knew where they might be? *If anything happens to Annie, I'll never forgive myself,* thought Warbucks. *I never should have let her leave with those two; I knew they were fishy characters as soon as I laid eyes on them! I might have signed Annie's death warrant. We* must *find her!*

Grace had the Dusenberg's engine running, waiting for Warbucks to come out. When he did, she stepped on the gas and the powerful automobile roared out of the driveway and into the streets, speeding downtown. Above their heads, the autocopter whirred, the Asp at the controls, and Punjab in direct radio communication with the Dusenberg. Around them, sirens shrieked as police squad cars flanked them and fanned out to take other avenues downtown.

Punjab had a pair of powerful binoculars with him, Swiss-made, with which he was scanning the city below, looking out for the 1929 Ford pickup, one lone needle in the haystack of a city of five million people.

"Punjab," Warbucks barked into the radio transmitter. "The bridges to New Jersey first!"

The autocopter turned in obedience to the command.

"He's got her now," remarked Lily as she saw Rooster coming back with Annie. He was still twisting her arm cruelly, forcing her to march double-time. "Well, we'll soon be rid of the brat. Good riddance to bad rubbish, I say."

"Where are we gonna dump her?" asked Miss Hannigan.

"In the river, of course."

Miss Hannigan's brow creased in a frown. "But she might drown!"

"Might drown!" hooted Lily derisively. "Get you! Might drown. Of *course* she'll drown. That's the plan, ain't it?"

"You mean Rooster is gonna *kill* her?" Miss Hannigan couldn't quite get that through her head.

"Well, I sure hope so," pouted Lily.

"*Kill* her? Really *kill* her?" She had never taken this into consideration as a possibility, and she obviously was having problems with the concept.

"Will you look at who called who dumb," snorted Miss St. Regis scornfully.

"He *can't!*"

"Ha! Watch him."

The bridges were a false lead, not one of them, or any of the ferry stations either, showing so much as a taillight of the pickup. But near the southern tip of Manhattan, where the trucking depots and warehouses are, near to the river, Punjab spotted something. He gestured for the Asp to fly lower, and the craft descended and hovered while Punjab fiddled with the fine adjustment on the binoculars. That looked like . . . it might be . . . it was!

"Sahib," Punjab spoke into his transmitter, "the truck is on Canal Street, heading south. Repeat, the truck is on Canal Street heading south."

"I read you, Punjab, loud and clear. Pursue and take whatever action is necessary. We are on course." Warbucks turned to Grace. "Floor it," he said tersely. The Dusenberg shot forward like the mechanical rabbit on a dog track. The needle on the speedometer went crazy. 80 . . . 85 . . . 95 . . . 100 miles an hour. Around him, sirens wailed as the New York Police Department and the G-men stepped up the chase.

They were all back in the pickup, heading south to the Battery, where the riptides could carry a body far out to sea and never bring it back. Miss Hannigan sat strangely silent, and this frightened Annie even more than Rooster's punishing grip on her arm. Her mind was racing; there must be a way out. There must!

They were in the most neglected part of the city. Nothing but old freight-train tracks and railroad bridges. Because there were virtually no cars here even in daylight, the roads had been permitted to fall into ruins, and the streets were a mess of potholes, bone-jarring bumps.

The pickup, with Lily at the wheel, jounced over the holes, throwing them around in the front seat, and slamming them up against the doors and the dashboard.

"Next time, Rooster," complained Miss Hannigan sarcastically, "find a hotel that can drive."

"Zip your lip, stringbean!" snarled Lily. Her arms were getting sick and tired of jockeying this behemoth around, and she was anxious to be on the boardwalk at Atlantic City, someplace warm and wonderful, sitting in a deck chair sipping champagne and wearing sunglasses.

Annie held her breath. An idea was forming in her mind, a last-chance idea that might possibly work. She began to squirm around in her seat.

"Excuse me, mister," she said to Rooster in a little-girl whine. "Can we stop a second? I gotta go." As Rooster didn't even bother to reply, Annie turned to Miss Hannigan. "I really gotta *go*, Miss Hannigan." Then, to Lily, "I mean it, lady, you're asking for it!"

Rooster, no mean con artist himself, and you can't con a conner, grabbed Annie by the front of her dress and, growling, shook her like a rag doll.

"Miss Hannigan!" yelled Annie, pressing her knees together as though an accident was imminent.

But Miss Hannigan was shaking her head. "It's a con. She's housebroken."

Nevertheless, Lily slammed on the brakes.

"Drive!" Rooster shouted.

But Lily was climbing down out of the cab.

"To Atlantic City? In a puddle? Not this little honey."

Annie saw her chance, the cab door was open. With a single jerk, she pulled herself out of Rooster's clutches and vaulted out of the truck. The check flew from Miss Hannigan's fingers, and sailed out on the draft that Annie had created. Grabbing it in midair, Annie made a dash for it, sprinting as fast as she could.

"Grab her, Rooster!" Miss Hannigan yelled needlessly. "She's got the check!"

"This is news?" snarled Rooster as he pelted after Annie.

Annie ran through the dark tangle of the tracks, feeling the rough ties cutting into her feet. She had no idea where she was going; this place was a jungle of railroad tracks and sheds. But up ahead of her was a bridge of some kind, reached by a perpendicular ladder. At least a truck couldn't follow her up the ladder, so she made for it.

143

Behind her, Rooster came running fast and low, murder in his heart. He had expected to throw the brat in the ocean long before they reached Atlantic City, but never mind that now; this place would do as well. He'd had it with her. The sooner the kid was dead, the better off they'd all be.

A steep and rocky right of way led to the ladder, and Annie scrambled up on her hands and knees, the sharp stones cutting into her tender flesh. She could hear Rooster gaining on her, getting closer with every second.

Lily drove the pickup as close to the bridge as she could. The two women peered into the darkness, seeing Annie and Rooster silhouetted against the sky, caught in the glare of the bridge lights.

"That's it," said Lily. "He's almost got his hands on her and when he does, bye, bye, Annie."

Without a word, Miss Hannigan climbed down from the truck and started after Rooster.

Annie was climbing the railroad bridge ladder now, making for the top. Below her Rooster's fingers had closed around the bottom rung. But she mustn't look down. She must look up to the top of the . . . oh, no!

What Annie had mistaken for a closed bridge was actually a drawbridge, the kind that splits open to let ships pass through underneath. And this unused bridge was locked open permanently. What seemed to be a ladder was actually railroad ties, upended. So, beneath her was a man who wanted to kill her, while ahead of her was . . . nothing. A void. Empty space. Climb to the top and there was nowhere to go but thin air, more than two stories up. She turned and looked down; Rooster was very close, she could see his ferrety eyes glinting with malice, and she knew that he'd show her no mercy. Once he caught up with her, Annie was done for.

No, there was nowhere to go but up, and fast. As she scrambled up the perpendicular section of track, she felt Rooster's hand grabbing for her ankle, missing, grabbing again, then it closed around Annie's ankle and clung. She was caught.

But then the hand fell away, and Annie looked down.

To her amazement she saw Miss Hannigan tugging at her brother's sleeve, pulling his arm down, freeing Annie.

"A loathsome child, no doubt about it," Miss Hannigan was saying, "a monumentally irritating, horrible, dreadful, obnoxious child, but that's not enough to kill her, Rooster, that's not enough to kill her."

Rooster turned around savagely and beat his sister's hands away from him. Then, with one punch, he knocked Miss Hannigan cold, and took off after Annie again.

The brief tussle had given Annie time to climb nearly to the top. She could feel the cold wind of the void rushing past her face, and she knew there was nowhere to run, nowhere to hide; she was doomed.

Yet she kept climbing, to the narrow top, to the thin edge of the span where the bridge yawned wide. It was only a matter of seconds before Rooster would be upon her, his hands would be around her throat, choking the life out of her. And yet she kept going, crawling out to the lip of the bridge, hanging on there, clutching tightly.

Above her, in the night, a faint noise grew louder. And louder. And nearer. She recognized the sound. It was the autocopter. *It was the autocopter!*

But how could they save her? All Punjab and the Asp could do was hover helplessly as Rooster caught up with her, grabbed her, reached for her throat. Even if Punjab used weapons, even if he had a gun with him, he would not dare to shoot for fear of hitting Annie. And he had no gun, only the pair of binoculars through which he watched the life and death battle going on below. Annie was kicking and struggling, the two of them were moving around dangerously close to the narrow edge where the bridge ended in midair, and Rooster was pushing, pushing. A body hurtled through the air as Punjab watched in horror. It was Annie.

She fell about eight feet. A steel bar was projecting from the bridge eight feet down, and Annie managed to catch hold of it. Now she was dangling precariously from the inner face of the bridge, her feet swinging over empty air and the river. And now she was more vulnerable than ever, right where Rooster could pick her off easily.

He scrambled down the ties until he was parallel with Annie, looking into her eyes. He had a ladder below him, while Annie had only empty space. She heard Rooster's snarling laugh, looked into his mean little eyes, and knew her last hour had struck.

Now Punjab had an idea, a risky one, but it just might work. Everything depended on the tensile strength of precious Indian silk, the stuff of which Punjab's turban was made. Hundreds of feet of it, woven lovingly by master craftsmen, and wound around and around, fastened with a ruby. Swiftly Punjab pinned the ruby to his tunic. Swiftly he freed the end of the turban and wrapped it many times around the passenger seat of the 'copter, tying it tightly. Now he opened the 'copter door and, holding tightly to the silk as a lifeline, began to lower himself into the air. The Asp maneuvered the craft so that it hovered as close to the bridge as he could come without crashing into it.

Today, helicopter rescues are commonplace, but then there were no precedents. Nobody had ever attempted this before, possibly because this was the first 'copter in existence. On the other hand, nobody today would be fool enough to lower a nine-foot, 400-pound man on a thin makeshift rope of turban silk.

Rooster reached his hands through the ties and found Annie's hands, still clinging to the steel bar. If he could force her fingers free, she'd plummet straight down, a hundred feet into the river. He began to tug at her small hands with his powerful ones. Annie felt her grip beginning to loosen.

"Hang on, Annie!" a voice shouted below her. It was Oliver Warbucks, who had arrived escorted by screaming sirens. "Hang on! Bring a net," he yelled to the police.

The turban silk that Punjab was clinging to stretched thinner and thinner. Above him the 'copter was being pulled off balance by his weight, with the Asp struggling to regain control of the craft.

There was no way that Punjab would reach her in time. Rooster was prying Annie's fingers loose from the bar, one by one and . . . there! One hand had come free, and now Annie was swinging over the river by only her other hand, panting with fear and exertion, dangling, dangling, the seconds of her life ticking away. Rooster's malicious fingers began working on hand number two.

But just as Annie was done for, Rooster was jerked off balance. It was Miss Hannigan, pulling from below. Furious, he kicked out at her, but that was a mistake, a bad one. The kick destroyed his balance completely, and he fell, screaming, into the net the police were holding at the base of the bridge. They slapped the cuffs on him, and threw Rooster into the paddy wagon, next to Lily.

But Annie was still in mortal danger. Her arm had been nearly pulled from its socket by her weight, and she was dangling so perilously that she couldn't bring her other hand up to share the weight. More than that, the air currents were twisting her around like a puppet on a string.

On the ground, Oliver and Grace watched helplessly, Grace sobbing openly, twisting her hands in fear. Warbucks' hands were knotted fists; his face was pale, and the muscles in his jaw stood out like clenched knots.

Annie's hand was slipping. It was all over.

But Punjab had reached her now. Punjab's arm was around her plucking her from the bar, holding her tightly.

"Oh, Punjab," Annie murmured, and let herself go limp in his arms, fainting.

"Do not sleep yet, Princess," said Punjab softly.

Annie's eyes were drifting shut. "I can't help it. I'm so tired . . . so very tired."

They hung by a gossamer thread of silk, over the river, over the city. It was so beautiful, to drift like this, in the safety of Punjab's arm.

But they were far from safe. At any moment the silk of the turban might snap, the threads parting, and plunge them both to a watery death.

"To pull us to safety, I need both hands. You must hold onto me," warned Punjab.

"I can't," whispered Annie. Every ounce of her strength had been used up in her ordeal with Rooster.

"Buddha says a child without courage is like a night without stars," said Punjab.

The words roused her. Never, never would Annie be called a child without courage. She rallied and managed to wind her arms around Punjab's neck and cling to him.

Hand over hand, inch by inch, the Indian giant climbed back up the silken rope and into the safety of the 'copter.

It was over. It was finally over. Annie was too dazed to believe it. It was only when she stepped out of the 'copter and into Oliver Warbucks' waiting arms that she began to feel safe, to feel loved, to feel as though she really, truly had a home.

CHAPTER FOURTEEN

I'm not sure you want to read about this part, because there are no villains, and there's no danger, no daring rescues out of the sky, no valiant orphans or nick-of-time warnings. There's only love and friendship and good times and—let's face it—that can be pretty dull to read about.

But if you like parties, well, you should have gone to the blowout Warbucks threw for Annie when the official adoption papers were finally signed, and Oliver Warbucks became "Daddy" Warbucks at last. That party was like the circus, the ballet, Radio City Music Hall, and Christmas all rolled into one. The New York Philharmonic played. Even the Rockettes came, after the last show at the Music Hall, and high-kicked and strutted to Annie's delight. There were elephants and clowns and monkeys, and Sandy wore a red-and-white ribbon around his neck and ate so much he got sick later.

There were fireworks that spelled out A*N*N*I*E in the sky in red, white, and blue letters, and FDR and Eleanor sent a telegram; they couldn't come because Eleanor was inspecting a coal mine and FDR was busy signing more bills into laws. But the president sent his chief aide, Harry Hopkins, and Mayor LaGuardia came himself.

Grace looked beautiful in a dress of sky blue that changed the color of her eyes, and a diamond ring on her left hand that sparkled nearly as brightly as her smile. And as busy as she was with the party, and as popular as she was with the guests, she would come over frequently to wherever Annie and "Daddy" were and hug them both.

Punjab and the Asp were heroes, and everyone wanted to hear about the daring rescue from the air, especially Miss Hannigan, who had heard it many times, and besides, she'd been there, hadn't she? But there was something about the way that Punjab told it that made her heart go flutter-flutter and, besides, she *loved* tall men. Miss Hannigan was at the party? Oh, yes, didn't I mention that? See, she was forgiven for everything because she really did help a lot in saving Annie's life, and that was the best recommendation to Mr. Warbucks' good graces. And it was decided that Miss Hannigan wouldn't be all that terrible if she had a job that wouldn't put her into contact with little girls. Ever. So they were working something out. Meanwhile, Miss Hannigan was living in a furnished room nearby, listening to her radio and drinking store-bought gin, but less of it than before.

Oh, and Pepper, Molly, Duffy, Tessie, Kate, and July never did go back to the Hudson Street Home for Girls, Established 1891. But you knew that already. You also knew that a new and enlightened director was appointed, and that the girls who remained behind were now well fed, well clothed, and learning French and tap-dancing. As for "our" orphans, they were all going to be adopted into rich homes by friends of Oliver's who wanted to be in on the latest thing. And if any of them got left out, Mr. Warbucks promised to adopt them himself.

Annie wore a dress of red velvet with a white collar, in the style she loved best, and danced with everybody who asked her. But most of all, she stayed by her new "Daddy's" side, holding tightly to his hand and dizzy with happiness. Around her neck she was wearing the golden locket he'd bought for her at Tiffany; and when he hung it around her neck the music played, the bells rang out and photographers snapped their pictures for the front pages of the newspapers.

Not that they were ever to live a quiet life. Oh, no, they would have many adventures over the years, and Annie would be brave and resourceful, just as you'd expect, and Sandy would always be by her side, and Punjab and the Asp somewhere nearby, in case the going got too rough for a little kid to handle. But they always had fun, good times or bad.

And it was some party.

After all the guests were gone and Annie had been tucked into the canopy bed in her room, Sandy curled up at her feet, she couldn't sleep. Too much excitement, probably. She lay there in the darkness, pleasantly weary, listening to the murmur of voices outside her door. She could make out some of the words . . . "she" and "Annie," and she knew that "Daddy" Warbucks and Grace Farrell were planning for her future.

And a little later, the door opened and she saw two people come in. She could smell a sweet perfume, and see a bald head gleaming in the light coming in from the corridor. A soft, fragrant hand touched her brow to see if she had a night fever (she didn't), and a man's hand touched her on the shoulder and pulled her blanket more tightly around her.

And Annie reached out with both her hands and caught the two hands in hers and held them.

And this time the Dream didn't dissolve.